Those Smith Boys
on the Diamond

Howard Roger Garis

THOSE SMITH BOYS ON THE DIAMOND

OR

NIP AND TUCK FOR VICTORY

BY

HOWARD R. GARIS

Safe at Home

THOSE SMITH BOYS
ON THE DIAMOND

OR

NIP AND TUCK FOR VICTORY

BY

HOWARD R. GARIS

Author of Uncle Wiggily and Alice in Wonderland, Uncle Wiggily Longears, Uncle Wiggily and Mother Goose, Uncle Wiggily's Arabian Nights

MADE IN U. S. A.

M·A·DONOHUE·&·COMPANY
CHICAGO NEW YORK

Made in U. S. A.

COPYRIGHT, 1912 BY
R. F. FENNO & COMPANY
Those Smith Boys on the Diamond

CONTENTS

CHAPTER

I	A Close Game
II	A Fire Department Run
III	A Leaky Boat
IV	A Great Home Run
V	Off For Westfield
VI	A Lively Hazing
VII	Moving the Senior Stone
VIII	Organizing the Nine
IX	Bill is Hit
X	The Doctor's Verdict
XI	Meeting an Old Friend
XII	Professor Clatter's Plan
XIII	Bill is Himself Again
XIV	The Try-Out
XV	The Conspirators
XVI	Caught
XVII	Bill's Pitching
XVIII	A Plot Against Bill
XIX	The Professor's Warning
XX	The Plotters Caught
XXI	An Interrupted Supper
XXII	Hitting a Bully
XXIII	The Fight

XXIV	The Kidnapped Pitcher
XXV	To the Rescue
XXVI	Just in Time
XXVII	A Scrimmage
XXVIII	The Glasses are Gone
XXIX	Mersfeld in the Box
XXX	Bill's Fall
XXXI	"Play Ball!"
XXXII	Nip and Tuck For Victory
XXXIII	Winning the Pennant

CHAPTER I

A CLOSE GAME

"Come on now, Bateye, soak it in!"

"Say, are you going to hold that ball all day?"

"What's the matter with you; didn't you ever see a horsehide before?"

"Oh, for the love of Mike! Throw it! Throw it! Do you want to give 'em a run?"

"That's the way! Wake up, Bateye!"

These were only a few of the expressions and questions hurled by the other players at Bateye Jones, the Freeport rightfielder, who, after running back to recover a ball that had passed high over his head, was holding the sphere for a moment until he had made sure of the position of the runner, Jake Jensen, of the Vandalia team.

"Throw it! Throw it! You can take a picture of it after the game!" howled Captain John Smith of the Freeport nine, as he danced about behind home plate, and saw Tom Evans come in from third, and noticed Jensen legging it around from second.

Bateye threw, and, mingling with the cries of the players and the yells of the crowd, there were groans of anguish as the ball passed high over the second baseman's head, who jumped for it in vain.

Bill Smith, the wiry little pitcher, made a successful grab for the horsehide as it bounced on the ground, captured it, and hurled it to third, just in time to catch Jensen there.

"Out!" yelled the umpire.

"Aw, say, I beat it a mile!" protested the panting runner. "What's the matter with you, Foster?"

"Out," said the umpire again, waving his hand to indicate that Jensen was to leave the bag.

"Say, I'll leave it to anybody if I—"

"Come on in," invited Rube Mantell, captain of the Vandalias in a weary tone, and Jake shuffled to the bench.

"Mighty lucky stop, Bill," called Pete, or "Sawed-off" Smith, to his brother the pitcher. The small-statured lad again took his position at short stop which he had left for a moment. "I wonder what's the matter with Bateye to-day? That's the second error he's made."

"Oh, I guess he got a bit rattled with so many howling at him," spoke Bill good-naturedly. "Come on now, Pete. There are two down, and we ought to wallop 'em easy when it comes our turn. Watch me strike Flub Madison out."

Bill, who was the best pitcher the Freeport team had secured in several seasons, again took his place in the box, while his brother John, or "Cap" from the likeness of his name to that of the old Indian fighter, resumed his mask, after shooting a few indignant looks in the direction of the unfortunate Bateye Jones.

"He's got to improve if he wants to stay on the team," murmured Cap Smith as he waited for the next ball. "I s'pose he'll excuse himself by saying the sun was in his eyes, or something like that. Or else that he can't see well in the daytime. He certainly can see good at night. Old Bateye—well, here goes for the next one," and Cap plumped his fist into the big mitt, and signalled to his pitching brother to send in a slow out curve to Flub Madison who took his place at the plate.

It was the ending of the eighth inning, and the score was seven to six, in favor of the Freeport lads. The game was far from won, for their opponents were playing strong, and still had another, and last, chance at the bat. To win meant much for the team on which the Smith Boys played, for they wanted to capture the championship of the County League, this being one of the last games of the season.

"One ball!" hoarsely called the umpire, as Bill unwound, and sent the horsehide sphere plump into the mitt of his older brother.

Cap looked an indignant protest, and hesitated as he tossed the ball back. It was as clean a strike as could be desired, but it was not the first time the official had favored Vandalia that day. The game was on their grounds, and the rivalry that existed between the two cities, located on either side of the Waydell river, was carried even into baseball.

"Make him give you a nice one, Flub," called some of his friends.

"He'll walk you, anyhow," added another sarcastically.

Bill Smith gritted his teeth but said nothing. He shook his head as his brother signalled for the same kind of a ball, and sent in a swift drop. Flub bit at it, and swung viciously.

"Strike one!" sounded sweet to the ears of the pitcher and catcher.

There was a vicious "ping" as the next ball was sailing over the plate, and for a moment the hearts of the Freeport nine and the hopes of their supporters were like lead, but they turned to rejoicing an instant later, as they saw the ball shoot high over the extreme left grandstand, and disappear.

"Foul strike!" called the umpire, as he tossed a new ball to Bill.

Cap signalled for the fast drop, and his brother nodded in assent.

"Three strikes! Batter out!" was yelled a moment later and Flub threw down his stick in disgust, and walked toward the outfield.

"Now's our last chance!" exclaimed Bill to John, as he came running in, while the teams changed places. "We ought to get at least three runs—in fact we need 'em if we're going to win, for they've got three of their best hitters up when they come for their last dips. But if we can get a lead of four runs we'll be all right."

"Yes, we'll be all right if Bateye doesn't go to sleep again," grumbled Cap. "Say, what's the matter with you?" he demanded as the unlucky rightfielder filed in.

Those Smith Boys on the Diamond

"Why—er I—that is I—"

"Oh, out with it! You're holding that talk as long as you held the ball. Don't do it again!" and Cap, who never could be ill-natured for very long, condescended to smile, while Bateye promised to do better in the future.

"Now Doc, show 'em how to make a home run," suggested Pete, as Harry or "Doc" Norton, dubbed with the medical term by virtue of his father's profession, came up to the bat. Doc tried hard, but only got a single. He was advanced to third when Norton Tonkin rapped out a nice two bagger, but that was as far as luck went for the Freeport nine that day. The next three players struck out under the masterly pitching of Nifty Pell, and the three Smith Boys did not get a chance.

"Well, we're one run to the good. If we can hold 'em down the game's ours," observed Pete, as he walked out with his brothers, followed by the rest of the team. "It's up to you, Bill."

"I know that, Sawed-off," was the answer. "I'll do my best, but I can't play the whole game. Crimps! But I *would* like to win this game! They've been making so many cracks about putting it all over us!"

"We've *got* to win!" said Cap Smith fiercely. "We need this to help us get the pennant. Don't get nervous Bill, and you can do 'em. Try that up shoot on Scurry Nelson."

The last half of the ninth inning began. There were agonized appeals from the Vandalia supporters for the nine to cinch the tying run, and then to bring in half a dozen more for good luck.

"They shan't do it, if I can help it!" murmured Bill Smith half-savagely, as he took his place.

Noticing the manner in which Bill stung in a few practice balls his brother behind the plate smiled happily.

"Bill hasn't lost any speed," he thought gleefully.

Scurry Nelson swung with all his force at the first ball, and his bat passed neatly under it.

"Strike one!" came from the umpire, as if it made no difference to him.

"Only two more!" howled the supporters of the Freeport nine. "You can do it, Bill!"

Bill tried the same kind of a curve again, and got away with it, but on the third attempt, after giving a ball on purpose, he heard the fatal "ping" and a swift grounder got past Pete.

There were groans of dismay from part of the crowd, accompanied by howls of delight from the other half, as Scurry landed on first. Bill felt his heart wildly beating, and Cap thumped his big glove viciously.

The Vandalia team on the bench was in transports of joy. Already they saw their enemies vanquished. Bill calmed himself by an effort, and even smiled as he faced Buck Wheeler the next man up. Buck was a notoriously heavy hitter and it seemed as if he would knock the cover off the ball when he swung at the first one Bill sent in. Only he didn't hit it.

And he didn't hit the next two, either, though he made desperate efforts to do so, and there was not quite so much elation on the faces of the Vandaliaites as the next man got up. He knocked a little pop fly, which Bill caught with ease making two out and, as quick as a flash the pitcher turned and threw to second, toward which bag Scurry was legging it for all he was worth. Bill was just a second too late, however and the runner was safe.

"Two down! Only one more, and the game is ours!" came the encouraging yells from the grandstand where the Freeport supporters were crowded.

Bill smiled happily and got ready for the next man, at the same time watching Scurry on second. The following player was Will Longton, and had a high batting average. There was a smile of confidence on his face as he stepped to the plate.

Bill sent in a puzzling twister, and Will smiled as he refused to bite at it.

"Ball," called the umpire.

"Take it easy! He's afraid, and he'll walk you," was the advice Will got. He was still smiling confidently when the next ball whizzed past him.

"Strike," came from the umpire, with obvious reluctance, since he wanted to see his friends win. Will looked an indignant protest at the official, and rubbed some dirt on his hands, so that he might better grip the bat.

"Watch him soak the cover off!" howled an enthusiastic admirer.

Longton did hit it, but only a foul resulted, and Scurry, who had started for third, had to come back.

"You know how to do it, Bill," called the catcher to his brother, giving him a sign. Bill nodded, and the next instant, amid a breathless silence a swift ball shot from his hand, straight for the plate.

With an intaking of breath Will Longton swung at it with such force that he turned completely around, and the look of astonishment on his face was mirth-provoking, as he realized that he had missed.

"Pung!" went the ball as it settled into the pit of Cap Smith's glove, and the voice of the umpire, as he called "Three strikes—batter out!" was lost in the howl of delight that welled up from grand stands and bleachers as the crowd realized that Freeport had held their opponents down in the last inning, and had won the game. What if it was only by one run? One run has often won a league championship.

"Great work, Bill!" cried Pete as he ran in, clapping his brother on the back.

"That's the stuff!" agreed Cap, as he hugged the pitcher. "We did 'em! Come on now, we can catch the next boat across the river if we get a move on," and the Smith boys, followed by the rest of the team, hastened to the dressing rooms, stopping only long enough to return the cheer which their opponents gave them.

The crowd was surging down from the stands, talking about the close game, discussing the best plays, arguing how if such a man had done differently the result would have been changed, and speculating as to Freeport's and Vandalia's chances for winning the pennant.

"What are you fellows going to do to-night?" asked Bateye Jones a little later as he stood talking with his chums, the Smith Boys on the little ferry boat which ran across the river from Vandalia to Freeport.

"Nothing special, I guess. Why?" inquired Bill.

"What do you say if we give the fire department a run?"

"Give 'em a run?" asked Cap with a puzzled air. "What do you mean?"

"Why they haven't been out in nearly two weeks, and they're just waiting for a chance to show off their new uniforms, and try the new chemical," spoke Bateye. "I say let's give it to 'em."

"How?" asked Pete, who detected a gleam of fun in the half-closed eyes of the lad who had such a habit of being out nights, and such a reputed ability to see in the dark, that it had gained him the name of Bateye. "How you going to do it?"

"Easy. Come over here, and I'll tell you. Come on, Doc, and you, too, Norton."

The two lads thus addressed, together with the Smith boys, moved forward on the little boat.

"I saw Spider Langdon and Beantoe Pudder looking at us," explained Bateye, when they were safe in a corner of the craft, "and I didn't want them to get on to us. Now here's my scheme. We can have some fun, and, at the same time give the department a chance to show off," and with that Bateye began to whisper the details of his plan.

It did not take long to disclose it, and at the conclusion he asked:

"Will you do it, fellows?"

"Will we? Will a cat eat warm milk?" demanded Pete, as if there was no question about it.

"But say, there won't be any come-back, will there? We got into trouble enough with the railroad people, and by flying our kite with Susie Mantell on the tail of it last year, so I'm not looking for any more," said Cap Smith solemnly.

"Oh, this will be all right," Bateye assured them. "Now I'll come over about eight o'clock, and make a noise like a tree toad. Then you come out. But lock up Waggles, your dog, or he might give the scheme away."

"We will," promised Bill, and then the boat tied up at the wharf, and the ball players in advance of the crowd rushed off.

"Say, I'll bet there's something doing," said Beantoe Pudder to Spider Langdon, as they followed the throng.

"Why?" asked the long legged lad, who was nicknamed "Spider."

"Because I saw those Smith Boys and Bateye talking together, and —" but at that moment Sam Pudder stumbled and would have fallen, had not his chum caught him.

"There you go again, Beantoe!" exclaimed Spider, as he helped him regain his balance. "What's the matter with you?"

"It's these new shoes, I guess," and Beantoe, who owed his title to his habit of stumbling, limped along. "But as I was saying, I saw the Smith fellows and Bateye and Doc talking together. There's something doing. Let's watch and see what it is," he concluded.

"All right, I'm with you. We'll hang around to-night, and maybe we can spoil their game," and the two cronies who, among other things in common, had a dislike for the Smith Boys and their friends, hurried along, whispering together.

Meanwhile the members of the Freeport Volunteer Fire Department were all unaware of the plot brewing against them.

CHAPTER II

A FIRE DEPARTMENT RUN

"WELL, boys, how did you make out at the game?" asked Mr. Smith, as his three sturdy sons tramped into the house a little later.

"Fine," answered Pete. "It was a close game, but we won."

"Good!" exclaimed the father. "I wish I'd been there."

"What's Mrs. Murdock got for supper?" demanded Bill, as he sniffed various odors coming from the kitchen. "I hope it's roast lamb!"

"I want sausage and potatoes!" cried Pete.

"Get out! It's too early for sausage," asserted Cap. "Guess again, Pete."

"What is it, Mrs. Murdock?" demanded Bill, as the housekeeper just then entered the room.

"Roast beef and baked potatoes," she answered, and there was a chorus of delighted howls.

"Fine!" cried Bill a second afterward making a rush for the buxom lady who had kept house for Mr. Smith, since his wife's death some years before. The other brothers, following Bill's lead, tried to kiss her at the same time, but she shut herself up in the pantry for refuge, and declared that they would not only be the cause of making the potatoes burn, but would also spoil the roast if they did not raise the siege. So they capitulated, and a little later were sitting down to a meal, with such appetites as only bless those who play ball.

And while the meal is in progress I will take the opportunity of introducing you to the Smith lads a little more formally.

There were three of them, as you have guessed, John the eldest, then William, or "Bill," as he was always called, and Pete, the youngest. They lived with their father and the housekeeper in a large, old fashioned house in the town of Freeport, on the Waydell river.

Across the stream was the town of Vandalia, and, as told in the first volume of this series, entitled "Those Smith Boys," there was much rivalry between the two places.

In the initial volume it was related how the Smith boys, who were always getting into mischief, but who did not mean to do wrong, started off a handcar, which ran away down grade on the new line of the Green Valley Railroad.

The handcar rushed through the railroad construction camp, knocked down a water tank, crashed into the tent of the chief surveyor, and made such a rumpus generally that the Smith boys, fearing the consequences, ran away.

It was a question whether the railroad would locate a station at Vandalia or at Freeport, and the decision was almost in favor of Freeport when the Smith boys, played their unfortunate trick. Then the chief surveyor determined to place the depot in Vandalia, out of revenge.

The Smith brothers had many adventures during the time they were away from home. They were looking for a thumbless man, whom they suspected of having robbed their father, and in their journeyings fell in with Theophilus Clatter, a traveling vendor of patent medicines, patent soap and a patent stain remover. They also met with Duodecimo Donaldby, who posed as a rain-maker, or a horse doctor, as suited his convenience.

The boys became traveling showmen to aid in the work of selling the patent medicine and soap, after their friend, Mr. Clatter, had been arrested for telling fortunes, and all the while the lads kept a lookout for the thumbless man.

How they found him, and overheard him discussing a plot to rob the paycar of the railroad, how they frustrated his plans, saved the car and won the gratitude of the railroad officials is told of in the book. Also how it was decided, as a sort of a reward for what the Smith boys had done, to locate the railroad depot in Freeport after all. So the thoughtless prank of the lads turned out well after all.

Part of the money stolen from Mr. Smith was recovered, and the boys also received a reward from the railroad company. Their father had planned to send them to Westfield Academy, immediately after their return from journeying about the country, but his financial and other matters prevented, so the boys had spent the winter helping him.

Mr. Smith's business affairs were now in good shape, and he was quite well off, so he determined that with the opening of the fall term at Westfield, his sons should attend there.

All summer the boys had been having a good time at various sports, of which baseball was chief. They were valued members of the Freeport nine, and it looked as though they would do more than their share in helping that team win the pennant. Only a few more games remained to be played before the season would be over.

"And then for Westfield," remarked Pete at the supper table that night, as they talked over their plans.

"I hope we can get on the nine there," said Cap.

"Oh, sure we can," declared Bill.

"Well, just because you can pitch well in the county league, doesn't say that you'll make good at Westville," objected Cap. "They play big college teams there, you know."

"Well, I'm not afraid of a college team," said his brother. "We'll make the nine—you see."

"Hark! What's that?" asked Pete suddenly, listening intently.

The sound of a tree toad came in through the opened window.

"Bateye Jones," murmured Cap.

"Are you boys going out?" asked Mr. Smith, looking up quickly from the paper he was reading, as he heard the name of the lads' chum.

"We—er—that is we thought of it," replied Bill.

"Well I do hope you won't get into any more mischief," went on their father. "I'm about tired of hearing everything that happens in this town laid to 'Those Smith Boys.'"

"So are we, dad!" exclaimed Cap. "And half of the things that are done aren't up to us at all."

"Well, perhaps that's so. But be careful now."

"Yes," they promised in a chorus, as they hurried out to meet Bat-Eye. And they really meant to do as they had said, but they were full of life and energy, and—well, you know how it is yourselves. Things don't always turn out as you think they will.

A little later six figures might have been seen hurrying away across lots in the rear of the Smith homestead. There had been some earnest whispering before their departure, and from the manner in which they hastened away it might have been argued, by anyone who knew the lads, that something was going to happen.

Then, a few seconds after the six had melted away in the darkness, two other figures rose up from the deep grass where they had been hiding.

"There they go, Beantoe," whispered one lad. "I wonder what's up?"

"We'll soon find out, Spider," was the response. "Come on, we can easily follow them."

Cautiously the two sped on in the blackness. Just ahead of them could be seen the group of six, and, from time to time, the twain could hear the voices of the Smith Boys, and their chums, Bateye Jones, Doc Lutken and Norton Tonkin.

"Can you hear what they're saying?" whispered Beantoe.

"Naw, but we don't need to. We'll just follow 'em."

The six led their shadowers quite a chase, and it was not until half an hour later that the foremost lad turned into a vacant lot that stood on the outskirts of the town. In the middle of the lot was a tumble-down barn and shed, long disused, and useful only as an abiding place for an occasional tramp.

"Gee whizz!" exclaimed Beantoe, as he and his crony sank down out of sight in the grass, for the six had come to a halt in front of the ancient structure. "Gee whizz! All this round-about way, when they could have walked down the road to this place in ten minutes."

"That's all right," argued Spider. "That shows that something is up. They didn't want to be seen coming here, and so they went around through the lots. Say, do you know what I think?"

"No, but I know what I think! I think we're chumps for coming after them! What does it amount to, anyhow?"

"I'll tell you," whispered Spider. "They have a secret society, and they hold meetings here. That's why they go about it so carefully. But they can't fool us. We're right here, and we'll sneak up, hear all they say, and then where will their secret society be, I'd like to know?"

"Do you really think so?"

"I'm sure of it. Look, they're going in the barn."

The two lads who were hiding in the grass, just beyond the fence that enclosed the old shed, raised their heads and looked. Surely enough the Smith boys and their friends were entering the deserted barn.

"Let's go up and listen," proposed Spider.

"No, wait awhile," advised Beantoe. "Give 'em a chance to get started, and we can hear all they say."

"They're making a light!" exclaimed Spider.

"Sure! Maybe they're going to initiate new candidates into their society. They think they're great stuff, but wait until they find out that we know all their secrets and passwords. Then they'll come down off their high horses."

"Sure! Come on up now. They must be started by this time."

Carefully getting up from their hiding places the two spies cautiously advanced toward the old barn.

"They're lighting up all over," observed Beantoe eagerly. "Must be going to have a regular celebration."

"I guess so. Come on over on this side. There's a little window that we can look in."

Spider was leading the way, and, just as he reached the window in question, his companion, as was his habit, unfortunately stumbled over a stone.

"Oh, there you go again, Beantoe!" exclaimed Spider wrathfully.

"I—I know it," admitted his crony. "Gee horse, but it hurts!"

"Well, keep quiet and come on. I guess—"

But what Spider guessed he never told, for at that moment there was a rush of figures from the barn, and the two spies were surrounded.

"We've caught 'em!" cried Cap Smith gleefully.

"Who are they?" asked Bill.

"I've got Beantoe Pudder," announced Doc Lutken, making a grab for the stumbling lad.

"And here's Spider Langdon," added Pete Smith, taking a tighter hold of the struggling youth.

"What were they doing?" inquired Cap.

"Following us, of course," said Norton Tonkin.

"We were not!" denied Beantoe, but the evidence was against him.

"I wonder what they want?" asked Bill.

"They must have known what we were going to do, and they want to squeal on us," suggested Bateye. "What shall we do?"

"Is it too late to stop it?" asked Bill, with a glance toward the barn.

Inside could be seen several flickering lights.

"Sure, it's going hard," answered Pete. "We can't put it out."

"Then let's make 'em stand for it," suggested Bateye. "They'll squeal anyhow, so let's make 'em take their share of the blame. It won't amount to much anyhow, for dad was going to have the place pulled down, and he won't care what happens to it. We'll tie Beantoe and Spider to the fence here, and run and give the alarm. The firemen will loosen 'em when they get here."

"Oh, don't tie us up!" pleaded Beantoe in alarm.

"No, don't leave us here!" begged Spider. "We'll never say a word about your secret society. Not a word, honest we won't!"

"Who said anything about a secret society?" demanded Bill.

"Why, ain't that what you came out to the barn for?" asked Beantoe.

"And did you follow us to hear the secrets?" inquired Pete, beginning to understand something.

Beantoe and Spider maintained a discreet silence.

"By Jinks! that's it, fellows!" cried Bill. "Say, this is rich! Tie 'em to the fence, and leave 'em. Then we'll give the alarm! Say, this is great!"

"Oh, don't tie us! We won't tell!" wailed Beantoe and Spider in a chorus.

But their foes were relentless, and in a few minutes the two spies were secured to the fence across the road from the barn. Meanwhile the flickering lights in the old structure had increased. Smoke was pouring from the windows and doors.

"There, you can tell any story you like now," said Pete, as he fastened the last knot. "Maybe they'll believe you and maybe they won't."

"Oh, we Smith boys will be blamed anyhow," was Bill's grumbling opinion.

"Then we might as well have the game as the name. Come on, it's going good now. We'll give the department something to do."

With a final look at the barn, and the lads who were tied to the fence, the Smith boys and their chums began to run down the road in the direction of the town. As they left, the whole interior of the rickety structure was lighted up, and the smoke poured out thicker than ever.

"They've set the barn on fire!" yelled Beantoe, as he struggled to get loose.

"And they're going to put the blame on us," added Spider, threshing about with his long legs.

"But we'll tell who did it!"

"What good will that do, when they find us here. Besides those fellows will give the alarm, and that will throw suspicion off them."

"But look how we're tied."

"I know it, but they'll say we did it ourselves. Oh, I wish we hadn't followed those Smith boys!"

"So do I!"

Swiftly running down the road, the boys in question, and their chums, set up a loud cry:

"Fire! Fire! Fire!"

They were on the outskirts of the town now, and the yell was soon taken up by many voices.

"Fire! Fire! Fire!"

"Where is it?" demanded several.

"The barn on my father's place," answered Bateye Jones pantingly.

Some one rang the alarm bell on the tower of the hose house.

The few firemen on duty began to rush about, and hitched up the horses. Other volunteers from nearby houses hastened to the hose house. A red glare could be seen reflected on the sky. The fire department at last had a chance for a run, and the members rejoiced in it, for there had been many days of inactivity. It mattered not that the barn was a worthless structure, better burned than left standing. It was a chance to get out the new apparatus, and must not be missed.

The hose wagon and chemical engine combined rattled out of the house. Men shouted various unimportant directions. The horses were scarcely awake.

"There they go!" exulted Bateye as he and the others prepared to race back to the scene they had so recently left.

"S'pose they find out we did it?" asked Pete.

"It doesn't matter," said Bateye. "I got leave from dad to burn the barn, only he didn't know I was going to do it to-night. He wants to put up a silo for cattle fodder on the place, so the barn had to come down, anyhow, and burning was the easiest way. But I thought we might as well have some fun out of it while we're at it."

"Sure!" agreed Cap Smith.

And then the boys, and scores of others, ran on, while voices multiplied the cry of:

"Fire! Fire! Fire!"

CHAPTER III

A LEAKY BOAT

THE old barn made a good blaze. Beantoe and Spider, tied with their hands behind them to the fence, could not help but admit that.

"Say, it's a peach of a fire all right!" exclaimed the long-legged lad, as he vainly struggled to free himself.

"It sure is! I wonder if they'll arrest us?"

"Of course not. If they did I guess Bateye and the others would be square enough to own up to it."

"I guess so, but maybe the firemen will be mad when they find out about it."

"Get out! They'll only be too glad of a chance to use the new hose. Besides Cooney Humpville hasn't used his new trumpet yet. Say, it's getting warm all right!"

"Yes, but it won't be any hotter. It's at the worst of the blaze now. Why don't the firemen come?"

"Here they are!" cried Spider.

From down the highway came a confused sound—shouts and yells mingled with the galloping of horses and the rumble of the hose wagon.

Up dashed the Freeport fire department, glorious in red shirts and red helmets, with the red hose wagon in their midst.

"Unreel the hose!" yelled the chief.

"Better take the chemical line in first, Cooney," suggested one of the red shirted men.

"Aw, don't call me Cooney; call me Chief!" begged the head of the fire-fighters. "I say put the hose on the hydrant and squirt."

Several men started to do this, but it was found that the nearest fire plug was farther away than the hose would reach, so it was unavailable for the fire.

"We've got to take the chemical, Cooney!" called another man. "Run the wagon nearer."

"Aw, don't call me Cooney, call me—" but his men did not stay to listen to his renewed pleading. The horses had been unhitched, and led away. Willing hands now dragged the wagon closer to the burning barn, and soon two lines of small hose to carry the chemical stream were unwound.

"Let her go!" yelled the men in a chorus, and the engineer who operated the tanks, screwed down the wheel valve that broke the bottle of sulphuric acid into the solution of soda and water.

Two foamy streams spurted from the hose nozzles, but it was easy to see that they would have little effect on the blaze. A lot of water was needed, and that was not available. Still, even though the old barn burned to the ground no harm could result. There were no other buildings within an eighth of a mile.

"Look here!" suddenly cried some of the firemen as they neared the fence, and then they discovered Beantoe and Spider tied to the rails.

"Who did it?"

"How did it happen?"

"Did you see anyone start the fire?"

"How did you get tied up?"

Questions were fired at the two lads, who were soon released. They looked through the gathering throng for a sight of the Smith boys and their chums. Beantoe saw Bateye laughing at him.

"There are the fellows who set the barn on fire!" cried the stumbling lad. "We saw 'em; didn't we Spider?"

"Sure; and they tied us up," and, forthwith the tale was related to such of the firemen and the crowd as would listen. And this was a goodly number, for it was seen that it was useless to try to save the barn, and all that could be done was to watch it burn, harmlessly.

"And those Smith boys tied you up?" demanded Chief Humpville, "and burned the barn?"

"Sure they did," asserted Bateye. "Them an' Doc an' Bateye."

"Just as likely as not these fellows set the barn, and tied themselves up," ventured a fireman, nodding at the captives.

"That's right; for the Smith brothers, and Bateye ran in and gave the alarm," added another.

"Didn't I tell you how it would be," wailed Spider. "I knew they'd blame us."

The twain protested, even unto tears, that they had no hand in the prank, and when they related, with much detail, how they had been surprised and caught the tide turned in their favor.

"You might know those Smith boys would be up to some such game as this," remarked Mr. Wright, who kept the feed store. "They ought to be arrested for arson."

"That's right; or else sent away to the reform school," added Mr. Henderson, who sold shoes.

"I hear they are going away to school this fall," declared Mr. Flint, a retired merchant.

"Well, they can't go any too soon to suit me," went on Mr. Wright. "They're always doing something—those Smith boys are!"

"But you must admit that they helped get the railroad to come here," suggested Mr. Blanchard, the grocer.

"Yes, but they're like a cow that gives a good pail of milk and then kicks it over," asserted Mr. Flint. "But I ain't going to stay here any more. The fire's most out, and I guess it's a good thing the old barn went. It was only good for tramps."

In spite of the usual feeling against the Smith boys this was the general sentiment, and when Chief Humpville wanted to make a charge of arson against the lads, he was persuaded not to.

"And so you fellows really did it; eh Bateye?" asked the chief, when the lad who could see in the dark had admitted his part in the affair, together with the Smith boys. They did it to clear Beantoe and Spider, who were deemed guilty by some.

"Sure I did it," admitted Bateye shamelessly. "Aren't you glad you had the run?"

The chief and his men were, but did not want to say so, for their new helmets and red shirts had been audibly admired, and the new apparatus, though its chemical streams were not effective against the fire, because of the start the blaze had acquired, were a source of pride to the townspeople.

"Ain't it against the law to set a fire?" demanded the chief, bound to maintain his dignity.

"Not when you have permission," asserted Bateye, "and my dad said I could get rid of the barn any way I liked."

"Did he say you could burn it?" asked the chief.

"Well, not exactly, but I liked that way better than any other, and so we did it. I knew nothing could happen, as there wasn't any wind."

The chief felt the uselessness of making any comments, especially as Mr. Jones was in the crowd, and confirmed what his son said.

"But I certainly didn't know he intended to burn it at night," said Bateye's father, "or I would have prevented him. However it's done, and I'm glad the barn is gone. And if the firemen think—"

"Oh, that's all right, Mr. Jones," said one of the red-shirts with a laugh. "We were getting too fat lying around. The run did us good."

It was not long ere the barn was but a heap of glowing embers and then the chief, calling hoarsely through his new trumpet, ordered the apparatus to "take up" though there was little to take up, and the department slowly went back to headquarters. The crowd followed, talking excitedly of what had happened.

"I guess you fellows won't take after us next time; will you?" asked Cap of Beantoe and Spider, as the two lads passed by.

"Humph! You just wait; that's all!" threatened Beantoe, vaguely. "We'll get square with you yet!"

"That's what," added Spider, striding along on his thin legs.

"They've got to think up something mighty soon," said Bill, as he and his brothers and their chums turned down a street that led to their homes. "We're going off to school in about three weeks."

"Not before the close of the ball season, though; are you?" asked Bateye anxiously. "We can't win the championship if you go."

"Oh, we'll finish out the season on the nine," promised Cap. "And I guess our team will win, if you don't make any more wild throws."

"Nary a one," promised Bateye fervidly.

It was several days before the town got over talking about the fire. Mr. Smith heard of the part his sons had taken in it, and talked severely to them.

"Why are you always up to such risky tricks?" he asked.

"This wasn't risky," declared Bill in justification.

"We didn't think it was any harm," added Pete.

"That's the trouble. You don't think enough. You didn't think the time you started the runaway handcar, and you remember what happened. Now be more careful."

They promised, and Mr. Smith, who was a very busy man, sighed and wished the boys would settle down and be less playful.

"Maybe when they get to the Academy, life there will help to settle them," he said with a shake of his head. Whether it did or not we shall soon see.

Meanwhile Beantoe and Spider were racking their brains for some plan to get even with the Smith boys and their friends.

"I don't care so much for Bateye and Doc. and Norton," said Beantoe, "but I would like to play a trick on Pete and his brothers."

"I'll see if I can't think of one," promised Spider. A few days later he came to his crony with joy written on his face. "I think we have them," he said exultingly. "There's a chance to put one over the Smith boys."

"How?"

"Come along, and I'll show you. They're going out fishing. I just saw Bill down to the hardware store buying some hooks, and I heard him tell Bateye they were going down past the swimming hole."

"Well, what's the answer."

"We'll stop at my house, get an auger and a loaf of bread, and I'll tell you on the way."

"What's the auger and bread for?"

"I'll show you. Come on. I want to get to their boat before they arrive. Then we'll hide and see some fun."

A little later Beantoe and Spider stole cautiously to the Smith boys' boat house on the banks of the Waydell river.

"You keep watch, and I'll bore the holes in the boat," suggested Spider. "It won't take long."

He was soon busy with the auger, and then his crony understood.

"I see!" he exclaimed. "You're going to make holes in the boat, and then when they're out fishing, it will sink!"

"Sure! You're a regular detective," said Spider, boring away while Beantoe watched.

"But won't the water come in as soon as they start out, and won't they get on to the trick," asked the stumbling lad after thinking it over.

"That's where the bread comes in," explained his friend. "I'll make a lot of holes, and stuff them up with bread. Then I'll smear dirt over the bread and it won't show. It will stay in the holes until Bill and the others get out in the middle of the river and then it will soak up, and come out. The boat will leak like a sieve, and they'll have to swim ashore."

Spider worked industrially, and soon had a number of holes in the bottom of the fishing skiff. The holes were well plugged with bread, and smeared over so that they did not show.

"Here they come!" suddenly warned Beantoe.

"Well, I'm done!"

Spider threw away what remained of the bread, put the auger under his coat, scattered to one side the pieces of wood that had resulted from the boring, and then he and his companion made a dash for the bushes, just as the three Smith brothers came in sight, with their fishing rods over their shoulders.

"Looks like a good day for bites," remarked Pete, as he got in the stern of the boat.

"Sure," agreed Bill, pausing on the bank to see if he had all his tackle.

"Get in, Bill, and I'll shove off," proposed John, for the boat was drawn partly up on shore.

"Now watch the fun," whispered Spider to Beantoe, as they peered from the bushes, and saw the boat being rowed toward the middle of the deep river.

"Maybe they'll be drowned," suggested Beantoe rather frightened.

"Those fellows? Naw! They can swim like fishes, but their clothes will get wet, and it'll serve 'em right for the way they treated us at the fire."

"How soon before the boat will begin to leak?"

"It ought to in a few minutes now. Gee whillikins! But I'm glad I thought of that trick! Won't they be surprised when the water comes rushing in?"

"They sure will," and then the two cronies eagerly watched the Smith boys, who, all unconscious of the fate in store for them, were rowing down toward the fishing grounds.

CHAPTER IV

A GREAT HOME RUN

"Wow!" suddenly exclaimed Bill Smith, as he gave a start that nearly upset the boat.

"What's the matter, did you jab yourself?" asked Pete.

"Yep. Ran a hook into my thumb," answered Bill, as he carefully extracted the barb, while Pete, who was rowing, rested on the oars and looked critically at the few drops of blood which oozed forth.

"Does it hurt?" he asked, rather needlessly.

"Does it hurt? No, I do this every day just for exercise!" retorted. Bill sarcastically as he put the injured thumb into his mouth.

"Shouldn't do that," observed Pete.

"Do what; jab myself? Don't you s'pose I know that, you amiable loon?"

"No, I mean put your bleeding thumb into your mouth. You are likely to get germs in it."

"In which, my thumb or my mouth?"

"Say, when you two fellows get through chinning, I wish you'd pass me down the box of hooks. I want to put on a smaller one," observed Cap, who was getting his line ready. As he spoke he looked down into the bottom of the boat, and asked:

"Who's been eating crackers here?"

"Crackers? Nobody," answered Bill. "Why?"

"Because there are a lot of cracker crumbs or bread crumbs under the seat here, and—"

Cap gave a sudden start, and looked toward shore. There was a slight movement in the bushes, and Beantoe and Spider who had been peering eagerly out, withdrew their heads into the shrubbery.

"The water must be coming in now!" exulted Spider.

"Sure!" agreed his crony.

Cap was anxiously staring at the bottom of the boat. He put his finger on a certain spot. The finger nearly went through a soft place, and a second later some water began trickling in.

"By crimps! I'm on to their game!" cried Cap. "Quick, fellows! Those cork floats from the box! Stuff 'em in the holes!"

"What holes?" demanded Bill, removing his thumb from his mouth that he might speak the more plainly.

"The holes Spider and Beantoe bored, and then stuffed up with bread," answered Cap. "It's an old trick. I suspected something when I saw the crumbs. They didn't clean 'em all up. Lively now! Cracky! Here's another hole. Hand over those corks, Pete, if you don't want to swim ashore. Quick now, and don't let those fellows suspect. We'll plug the holes, and go on as if nothing had happened. Lucky we've got plenty of corks."

"Hey! There's a lot of water coming in here!" called Bill.

"Keep quiet!" ordered his elder brother. "Plug it up. Don't let on that there's anything wrong. Beantoe and Spider are on shore watching us. I just saw the bushes moving, and there's no wind, so they must be there. Say, are you going to be all day with those corks, Pete?"

Thus livened up Pete passed back the box of bottle-stoppers. By this time the bread in several holes in the boat had become soaked through, and the water was coming in at a lively rate. But Cap and his brothers worked fast. They could see by the little bulges, caused by the swelling plugs of bread, where the holes were, and, soon they had them all stopped up before enough of the river had entered to do any harm.

Those Smith Boys on the Diamond

"Now row on, Pete," ordered Cap. "I guess we went them one better this time."

"Say, my feet are getting damp," objected Pete, for there was a little puddle of water under his seat.

"Pity about you!" sneered Cap. "If it hadn't been for me thinking of these corks you'd be wet all over. Row on, now, and when we get around the bend where those fellows can't see us, we'll sponge out. They'll be wondering why their trick didn't work. Row on!"

And, as Pete rowed, sending the boat along the river, it was watched by two very much puzzled lads on the bank. They wondered why the boat didn't sink.

"Say, I thought you said they'd have to swim ashore," observed Beantoe rather contemptuously to his crony.

"They will, in a minute. Maybe I pressed the bread in too hard, and it takes a while to soak up. But the boat will sink in a few seconds."

They resumed their watching, and, though they saw the three brothers doing something in the boat, the hidden ones never dreamed that the Smith boys were plugging up the holes with corks.

"It's got to sink pretty soon now, if we want to see the fun," observed Beantoe, after an anxious pause.

"I think it's going down some," said Spider doubtfully, wondering whether he had not worked the scheme right.

"Yes, it's going down stream, to the fishing hole," spoke Beantoe. "I guess it's all up with the joke."

They realized that it was all over as far as they were concerned a few minutes later, when the boat containing the Smith boys passed around the bend and out of sight, apparently in as good a condition as it had ever been, and not leaking a drop.

"Well, what do you know about that?" demanded Spider, as he got up and stretched his cramped legs, for they had been crouching in the bushes.

"What do I know about it?" demanded Beantoe in accents of disgust. "I know that you don't know how to play a joke; that's what I know. I thought we'd see some fun, and watch those fellows have to swim ashore."

"So did I, but—but something went wrong, or else they got on to the game, and stuffed up the holes," answered Spider, helplessly scratching his head. "Come on, I'll treat you to a chocolate soda."

This somewhat consoled Beantoe, but there was anguish in the hearts of the cronies when, that evening, as they were down at the post office with the usual crowd of boys, the Smith brothers, who had returned from a successful fishing trip, stepped up to the plotters.

"Here's something for you and Spider, Beantoe," remarked Cap, holding out his hand.

"What is it?" demanded the stumbling lad, backing away, for he feared a trick.

"Something to stop up holes in boats," answered Cap, as he showed a lot of corks.

There was a chorus of laughs for the Smith boys had told the story, and the joke was distinctively on Beantoe and his crony. They slunk away, and Spider had to stand treat for several more sodas before his chum would forgive him for being led into a plot that was so easily turned against themselves. It was some time before they again ventured to play a joke on our heroes.

Meanwhile the baseball season was drawing to a close, and the championship of the county league lay between Vandalia and Freeport. It came to the final game, the play-off of a tie.

"Now fellows," remarked Cap, one afternoon, as they journeyed toward the diamond in Freeport, where the closing contest was to take place, "we've just got to win to-day. It means the pennant for us."

"And for Vandalia—if we lose," added Pete, in a low voice.

Those Smith Boys on the Diamond

"But we're not going to lose, Sawed-off!" exclaimed Bill, as he swung his pitching arm around to limber it up. "Are we, Cap?"

"Not much," and the tall lad thumped his big mitt. "Don't let anything get past you to-day, Pete."

"I won't. Is Bateye going to play?"

"Yes, but he's improved a whole lot. My! There's a big crowd out!" added Cap, as he neared the grounds and saw the great throng on the stands, and scattered about the field.

"Hear 'em yell," remarked Bill.

"Yes, Vandalia is out for blood to-day. Lucky we won the toss, and have the game on our grounds. It's a good part of the battle."

The Smith boys were soon out on the diamond with their teammates, doing some hard practice. The crowds increased for not only was there an intense baseball fever in both towns, but, because of the natural rivalry between the places, a game between Freeport and Vandalia, always brought out a record-breaking attendance.

"Play ball!" called the umpire, and the game was on.

It was a hot contest from the very beginning, when Rube Mantell of the Vandalias knocked out a two-bagger with the first ball Bill delivered.

"Oh wow! Pretty one! Pretty one!" yelled the crowd. "That's a beaut! Take third! Take third!" shouted some enthusiastic one, but the ball was fielded in too quickly.

There was a grim look on Cap's face as he gave the signal to his brother in the box, and Bill nodded. He struck out the next man, who was a heavy hitter, gave the following player his base on balls, and struck out the third. The succeeding man knocked a hot liner which Pete, at short, stopped, almost at the risk of his life, and a goose egg went up in the first frame for Vandalia.

"Oh, not so bad; eh?" asked Cap, as Bill came in to the bench.

"No, but I nearly had heart disease when Rube whacked it that first time."

"Aw, that was an accident. He can't do it again."

Then Freeport went to bat and succeeded in getting one run over the plate, much to the joy of her supporters. Vandalia duplicated this in her second chance, and the game ran along to the seventh inning without another run being chalked up.

"Here's where we do something," announced Jake Jensen, of the opposing team, as he took his place, and swung his mushroom bat menacingly. But he only fanned the wind, as did his successor.

Then Flub Madison knocked as pretty a three-bagger as was seen in many a game, and before Bateye could get the ball in, the runner was speeding away from the last bag. But, as he turned, Doc. Lutkin who was covering third, limped to one side with an expression of pain on his face.

"Flub has spiked Doc!" yelled Pete, running over to his friend. The ball bounced in front of Doc, and Pete caught it, but Flub had seen it coming, and was back on the bag. "You spiked him on purpose!" cried Pete, drawing back his fist.

"I did not!" asserted Flub angrily. "He got in my way! I couldn't help it!"

"I saw you do it on purpose—you want to kill off our men!" went on Pete menacingly, and there might have been a row, had not Cap run down from home, and quieted his brother.

"I'm sorry," said Flub contritely. "Are you much hurt, Doc?"

"Oh, I—I guess I can play," answered the plucky lad, "but I can't run."

"We'll let you have a runner," proposed the captain of the Vandalia nine. It was the least he could do. Doc's foot was punctured in the fleshy part, and, after it had been treated, the game went on. Flub came in on a little fly by Nifty Pell, and that put the Vandalias one run ahead whereat there was great rejoicing.

"We've got to do 'em now or never," declared Cap grimly, when he and his mates came up for their turn.

They tried hard, but fate was against them, though Bill was called out at first on a close decision which even the crowd characterized as "rotten."

But it stood, and when that inning was over the score was two to one, in favor of Vandalia.

"Well, we have one more look in, and then—" Cap paused suggestively.

"I can see that pennant going across the river," announced Bateye gloomily.

"Say, you never were any good at seeing things in the daytime," declared Bill. "You want to take another look, Bateye. We're going to win!"

There was a positiveness in Bill's tones that seemed to infuse itself into the spirits of his teammates. There was a brief consultation among the Freeport players, and exhortation from the captain and manager, and then the final inning began.

Vandalia played desperately—played for blood, and got it—in the shape of one run, putting them two ahead. It was due to an error of the centre fielder, who slipped when he had a nice fly in his hands, and there was a groan of anguish. Then the Freeport players settled grimly down, and Bill struck out three in succession.

"Three runs to win!" said Cap in tense tones as he took off his mask and chest protector. "We've just got to get them."

Pete brought in one, and after a desperate race when he was nearly caught on third, Norton Tonkin landed another, sliding home in a cloud of dust when the third baseman threw the ball to the catcher, just above the latter's head, which error tied the score.

"Now for the winning run!" said Pete, as his elder brother went to the bat. But the chances were against the Freeport team getting it, as there were two out, and the Vandalia pitcher was lasting well. Still the score was tied and there would be another inning if Cap did not make good.

"But I'm going to bring in a run," he told himself grimly, as he rubbed some dirt on his hands, and took a firm grip of the stick.

The ball came whizzing toward him. He was half minded to swing at it, but a signal he had caught passing between the pitcher and catcher warned him, and he let it pass.

"Strike!" called the umpire. Cap opened his mouth to say something, and then thought better of it.

"You won't fool me again," he called to the man in the box, with a grim smile.

"Whack!" That was Cap's stick meeting the horsehide. Out sailed the sphere, a long, low straight drive into right field—away out among the daisies.

"Oh, wow!"

"Oh, pretty!"

"Oh, a sweet one!"

"Run, you old war-horse! Run, you scob! Run!"

"A homer! A homer!"

"All the way round! Come on in!"

These were some of the yells that greeted Cap's performance. But he did not stay to listen to them. On he sped for first and rounded the initial bag with a swing that carried him well on to second.

On and on he went, running as he had never run before since he felt that on him now depended the championship.

"Run! Run you lobster!"

"Run, you dear old goat!"

"Run, Cap, run!"

"Come on, boy! Oh, a pretty one!"

The grandstand was rocking and swaying with the stamping of feet. The cheers were deafening. The Vandalia players were almost stupefied. The Freeporters were dancing up and down in a wild delirium of joy.

The rightfielder was running after the ball like mad. He had picked it up. He was throwing it in. Cap was speeding toward third. He had passed it when the fielded ball was in the air. Could he beat it home?

That was what everybody wanted to know. On and on ran the player. Nearer and nearer came the ball. The second baseman had it now. He threw it toward the Vandalia catcher, who, with feet well braced apart was waiting for it with outstretched hands.

Cap was almost exhausted. His legs felt like wooden ones, but they kept going like the pistons of an engine.

"Come on, boy! Come on! Come on!"

"Oh you Cap!"

"Beat it! Beat it!"

Cap dropped like a shot and slid, feet foremost. The catcher reached forward. There was a vicious "ping!" as the ball landed in his big mit.

There was a moment of intense anxiety. A cloud of dust hid catcher, runner and umpire from sight.

And then, from this mist of dirt, in which three figures could dimly be seen moving about, came this one word:

"Safe!"

Oh, what a howling there was! What cheers, what yells, what thumpings on the back, what improvised war-dances, what shakings of hands!

For Freeport had won, almost on the last chance and had the pennant. No wonder Cap Smith was overwhelmed with praise as he walked panting to the bench.

"Say, I guess there's something in those Smith boys after all," remarked Mr. Flint, who had torn his score card to bits as he wildly whooped himself hoarse while watching the home run.

"Well, they might be worse," conceded Mr. Henderson.

CHAPTER V

OFF FOR WESTFIELD

WHETHER it was because their trick of putting holes in the Smith boys' boat did not work, or because they wanted to get even with the brothers on general principles was not made clear, but certain it was, that a few days after the closing ball game, Beantoe and Spider made another attempt to perpetrate something on our heroes.

"This time it will come off all right," Spider had assured his crony.

"It ought to; we spent time enough on it," said the stumbling lad. "I certainly hope it does."

With much labor and secrecy the two conspirators had made a lot of sharpened stakes, and tied stout cords to them. They had also prepared a quantity of molasses and lampblack.

"We'll wait until they're in their 'coop,' holding a meeting," explained Spider. "Then we'll drive these stakes in the ground at the foot of the stairs, so they'll trip over the strings when they rush down. And if they fall into the lampblack and molasses, we can't help it; can we?" he chuckled.

"Of course not," answered Beantoe, with a malicious grin. "But how are you going to get them to rush out of the coop?"

"Oh, I'll show you."

"And s'pose they catch us at it?"

"I don't believe they will. It won't take but a couple of minutes to stick in the stakes. The ground's soft and the stakes are sharp. We'll work it to-night, for it will be good and dark, and I heard Cap tell Bateye and Doc. to come over after supper, so they'll all be there."

"Good. We'll get square this time."

A little later two figures, carrying some stakes and a can, might have been seen proceeding cautiously toward the Smith homestead. The two figures did not go boldly up and ring the front door bell. Instead they sneaked around in the rear where there was an old workshop, which had been converted by Cap and his brothers into a sort of "coop" or den, where they held meetings and talked over pet schemes.

Entrance to the coop was obtained by means of an outside stairway, which led to the second floor, where the meetings were always held, in a room, the walls of which were hung with bats, masks, fencing foils, boxing gloves, fishing poles and other trophies dear to boyish hearts.

It was at the foot of this outside stairway, after carefully looking about to see that they were not observed, that Beantoe and Spider began thrusting the sharpened stakes into the ground. Then they wound the stout cord in and out among them, making a maze of string, which, if anyone ran into unexpectedly in the dark, would be very likely to trip him up.

"There, now to spread the molasses and lampblack around and give the alarm," said Spider, when they had nearly finished their preparations.

"Are you sure they're up there?" asked Beantoe.

"Pretty sure. You can see the light, and I heard a lot of voices."

They listened a moment and caught the unmistakable tones of Cap Smith.

"It's all right," whispered Spider. "Pour the stuff out, Beantoe."

"Aw, I don't wanter. You'd better," objected the tripping youth.

"I will not! Didn't I get all the stuff, and stick in most of the stakes?"

"Well, I sharpened some. Besides, I'm afraid if I pour it I might slip and fall into it."

"That's so, I didn't think of that," and as Spider recalled the unfortunate habit of his crony he took the can of molasses and lampblack from him, and began making a trail of it all about the foot of the stairs, walking backwards so as to keep out of it himself.

"I guess that will do," announced the long-legged lad at length. "Now we'll hide back here and watch the fun. I'll bring 'em out."

"How?"

"Listen, and you'll hear."

Spider drew from his pocket a blank cartridge pistol. Looking as well as he could in the dark, to observe that his companion was hidden, Spider fired two shots in the air, and immediately gave a very good imitation of a dog's agonized howling.

"They'll think it's their dog, Waggles," whispered Spider, "and they'll come out quickly enough."

His surmise was correct. The door of the coop, at the head of the outside stairway was suddenly thrown open, and in the glare of light could be seen Cap Smith standing.

"What is it?" the hidden ones could hear those in the coop asking. "Is Waggles shot?"

"Can't be Waggles—he's here," answered Cap. "Come back!" he ordered as the dog, with a whine, started down the stairs.

"But it was some dog," insisted Pete, coming to the door, and joining his brother as he peered out into the darkness.

"Sure it was—and two shots. I'm going down to see."

"I'll come too," volunteered Pete.

"I told you I'd get 'em out," whispered Spider, and Beantoe grunted.

Cap started down the stairs, followed by Pete. Bill together with Doc. and Bateye came after them.

"Now watch carefully!" whispered Spider, trying not to laugh.

Suddenly Cap uttered an exclamation. He had run into the first string. He swung about, got tangled in another and went down, for his feet slipped in the molasses.

"Great Scott!" he cried. "Look out, fellows, there's something wrong here! Keep back!"

But his warning came too late. Pete made a jump to help his brother, and he too went down, sprawling in the sticky stuff.

"It's glue!" he yelled. "Show a light!"

"What's the matter?" demanded Bill.

"Get a light," repeated Sawed-off, as he floundered about.

"Keep back!" yelled Cap.

There was so much confusion that Bill, Doc, and Bateye came down to see what the trouble was. Then, they too, got tangled in the cords, and went ingloriously down, the sticky and black stuff getting all over their clothes, hands and faces.

"Oh wow! This is awful!" panted Cap, as he crawled out, and being now able to dimly make out the cords and stakes he could avoid them. "It's a trick!" he cried.

"Time for us to skip," murmured Spider who was doubled up with laughter. "I guess this one works all right; didn't it Beantoe?"

"It sure did. But come on, or they'll catch us."

They started to crawl away. Cap staggered up the stairs and got a lantern. He came down, and by the light he saw what sorry looking objects were his brothers and chums.

"Oh, this is fierce!" he wailed.

"You're a peach!" cried Pete. "Look at him, Bill!"

"We're *all* covered with the stuff!" exclaimed Bateye, who looked like an amateur minstrel.

"Hark!" whispered Cap.

The sound of some one stumbling in the bushes came to the ears of the brothers. It was the unfortunate companion of Spider, falling down.

"Beantoe Pudder!" cried Cap. "He and Spider did this!"

He made a dash in the direction of the sound. Beantoe got up and tried to run, but went down again, dragging Spider with him, for the latter's long legs got tangled up in a garden rake.

"Come on!" cried Cap to his brothers after a rush as he stood over the conspirators. "I've got 'em both!"

They tried to arise, but Cap pushed Beantoe back, and grabbed Spider. He knew it would take the stumbling lad some time to get up, and before he could do so, Pete was on hand, and had made a prisoner of him.

"Both of 'em!" exulted Bill, who came up on the run. "What shall we do with 'em?"

"Give 'em a dose of their same medicine," decided Cap grimly. And it was done.

When the unfortunate Beantoe and Spider were released from the hands of their enemies they were even sorrier looking objects than were the Smith boys and their chums. For the work of rolling the conspirators in the lampblack and molasses had been thoroughly done, whereas our friends only had some scattered spots on themselves.

"Oh, let us go!" begged Beantoe, "we'll never do anything to you again!"

"Yes, please let us go, and we'll always be your friends forever," promised Spider eagerly.

"Not much you won't be our friends!" declared Cap. "We wouldn't let you be friends even with our dog, Waggles. Now, fellows, into the ditch with them, and I guess that will end it."

"Oh, don't!" wailed Spider.

"Please don't!" begged Beantoe. But no heed was paid to their protests, and into the ditch at the end of the garden they were thrown, from whence they clambered, dripping with slime, and very much chastened in spirit.

"But they certainly did put one over us," admitted Bill, a little later, as he and his brothers and chums were cleaning themselves off as best they could.

"Yes, and even though we got back at them, it won't take the molasses out of our clothes," said Pete ruefully.

"Maybe Mrs. Murdock won't make a fuss!" observed Bill uneasily, and the housekeeper did, even to the extent of complaining to Mr. Smith.

"Now, boys, this practical joke business has got to stop," said their father, when he heard the story next morning. "Spoiling your clothes is too much."

"But, dad," objected Cap, "it was Beantoe and Spider who worked it on us. We didn't do it!"

"Well, they wouldn't have done it if you hadn't done something to them first."

"No," protested Bill, "they were mad because the boat trick didn't work."

"And they tried that scheme on you because of what you did to them at the fire," remarked Mr. Smith. "No, boys, it must stop; and to make sure of it, I'm going to send you away."

"Send us away?" faltered Cap.

"Yes. It's the only means by which I can have any peace. I know you don't mean any harm, but I never know what is going to happen next. I have arranged for you to go away to boarding school—the Westfield Academy, as you know. The term does not open in two weeks, but I can't stand this any longer. Mrs. Murdock, help the boys to pack up. I'm going to send them to school at once, and have them out of the way. I have been thinking of this, and I wrote to Dr. Burton, president of Westfield, asking if they could come. He said they might, so get ready to go, boys."

Mr. Smith tried to speak severely, but there was a half smile on his lips. The boys said nothing for a few seconds. Then Cap softly cried:

"Hurrah for Westfield!"

"I'm afraid I haven't quite made the punishment fit the crime," said Mr. Smith softly, as he turned away. "But off you go, boys. You'll start to-morrow, and I hope you will like it. You may be a bit lonesome at first, but it will give you a chance to get acquainted with the school and grounds before the other students arrive. Now I'll have a little quietness," and Mr. Smith went to his library, while the boys executed a noiseless war dance.

"Oh, those boys! Those boys!" exclaimed the housekeeper throwing up her hands hopelessly.

How they managed to get ready on such short notice the brothers hardly knew, but they accomplished it, and the next afternoon, having bidden their friends good-bye, they took the train for Westfield Academy, an institution of learning about one hundred miles away.

"Now remember," called Mr. Smith after them, "no more practical jokes."

"That's right," promised Cap. "We're going to play baseball as soon as the spring season opens."

CHAPTER VI

A LIVELY HAZING

"Wow! But this is a lonesome place!" exclaimed Cap Smith, as he and his brothers were set down by the depot stage in front of the gates of Westfield Academy.

"And we've got it all to ourselves for two weeks," added Pete. "I wonder how we can stand it?"

"Got to," declared Bill grimly. "Say, they've got a beaut diamond," and he motioned toward the baseball field.

"Nothing doing in that line until spring," commented Cap. "Football has the call now, but I don't s'pose we'll get a look in at that. Well, come on," and he went through the massive bronze gates.

"Where you going?" demanded Bill.

"Up to see Prexy. Dad gave me a letter for Dr. Burton, the president, and we want to pay our respects, and find out where we're going to sleep to-night. I don't exactly feel like camping out on the grass."

"Me either," came from Pete. "Say, as soon as we can get into some old togs can't we get up a game. Maybe there are some fellows sent on here early, like us, and we can pick up a nine."

"I'm afraid not, son," spoke John, "but that looks like a place where a college president would hang out. Come on, we'll give it a trial."

A little later they were shaking hands with the venerable Dr. Burton, who made them genially welcome, but looked all the while as if he didn't quite know what to do with them, and wished they would take themselves off, or go away so that he could get back to a volume of Chinese proverbs on which he was working, making a translation of it into modern Hebrew.

"I'm very glad to see you young gentlemen," he said, "and I hope you will like it here at Westfield. The students will—ahem—arrive shortly." That was all the reference he made to the fact that our heroes were sent on ahead of the time as a sort of punishment, and the boys were duly grateful.

"I have arranged for you to have rooms, temporarily, in the senior dormitory," went on Dr. Burton. "Professor Landmore, the science instructor is there, and he—er—he will, ahem—look after you," and the good doctor seemed a trifle embarrassed.

"I guess he thinks we sure do need looking after," murmured Pete, when he and his brothers had settled down in a big room containing three beds, which apartment was to be their home until the term opened.

"Shall we decorate?" asked Bill.

"What, put up all our trophies? Not much!" exclaimed Pete. "Wait until we get into our own flat, and see what sort of neighbors we have. This will do for now. I'm going to get unharnessed," and he proceeded to don some more comfortable clothes than those in which he had traveled.

A little later the brothers were out on the deserted diamond, tossing balls back and forth, and batting them. In vain they looked for some one with whom to organize even half a nine, and finally they gave it up, and strolled about, looking at the college buildings, walking over the football gridiron, and speculating as to what sort of fellows they would get chummy with when the students arrived.

For two weeks our heroes lived rather a dull life, though Professor Landmore made friends with them, and took them on long walks collecting science specimens. Once he went fishing with them, but he paid little attention to the sport after he had captured a new species of frog, notes concerning which he proceeded to enter at great length in a book, while the Smith boys pulled out some fine specimens of the finny tribe.

That night, the final one before the opening of the term, our friends were given their regular rooms in the Freshman dormitory—three connecting apartments, not very large, but just suitable for the boys.

And straightway the brothers began to decorate the walls, each in his own peculiar way.

With their choice possessions and trophies hung up, the brothers gathered in Pete's room that night for a talk before turning in.

"Well, the crowd will be here to-morrow," observed Bill.

"Yes, and then for some lively times," added Pete.

"How do you mean?" asked Bill.

"Initiations, and hazing and all that. But we'll have to stand it."

"Surest thing you know," declared Cap. "We all want to make the ball team this spring, and if we balk out of the hazing I know what that means."

"Are you going to take all that comes?" asked Bill.

"Well, up to a certain point, but if it gets too strenuous, I'll take a hand myself. But we can't tell until the time comes. Now let's get to bed."

Lively were the scenes that took place the next day. With the arrival of many new students, the return of old ones, the assigning of the boys to their rooms, the making up of classes, it is a wonder that poor old "Prexy'" did not desert. But he took everything calmly, and soon a sort of order came out of chaos.

The Smith boys found themselves in the midst of a lively colony of students in their dormitory. There were five rooms on a short corridor, and of these our heroes had three. Pete's apartment was between those of Bill and John's, while the letter's adjoined the room of Donald Anderson, a new lad who was at once dubbed "Whistle-Breeches" by some senior from the fact that Donald wore corduroy trousers, which squeaked or "whistled" as he walked. As soon as he learned why he was so christened, he got rid of the offending garments, but the name stuck, and "Whistle-Breeches" he remained to the end of his course.

Next to Bill there roomed a well-dressed, supercilious lad, who was reputed to be quite wealthy, and his overbearing manners added to this surmise. He was James Guilder, but he was at once christened "Bondy" for he had boasted of his father's stocks and bonds.

Behold then, these five lads domiciled together in the Freshman corridor. Across the hall from Pete's room, was a larger apartment, which, as befitted his station, held a lordly senior, one Dick Lawson, who rejoiced in the name of "Roundy" because he was fat. He was also good natured, and though the school authorities had placed him there to have a sort of leavening effect on the Freshmen, he was too good natured to be any sort of a monitor.

After the first supper, partaken of with the entire school assembled in the refectory, the three Smith boys went to their rooms, not knowing what else to do.

"I say, we're not going to stay in like chickens; are we?" demanded Bill.

"No, but take it easy," advised Cap. "We want to get the lay of things before we start anything."

"That's all right," agreed Pete. "Do you know what the Freshmen do the first night?"

"Get hazed?" ventured Cap.

"No, they go out and collect signs from around town—pull 'em off, you know; bootblack signs, restaurant signs—any kind—and decorate their rooms with 'em. Let's do it. Whistle-Breeches said he'd go."

"Let's don't," came from Cap calmly. "To-morrow will do as well, and I want to look over some lessons. We've got to buckle down to work here. It isn't like the school at home."

"Wow! I say you're not going to become a greasy grind so soon; are you?" demanded Bill in contempt.

"Not exactly," answered Cap, "but we didn't come here just to have fun. Dad expects something of us."

"Of course," agreed Pete, "and we won't disappoint him, either. I guess I'll—"

But a knock on the door interrupted him, and a voice called out:

"Open up, Freshies!"

"The hazers!" whispered Bill. "Shall we stand 'em off?"

"Might as well get it over with," suggested Cap. "Just stick together, that's all, and when I give the word, which I'll do if they get too strenuous, just sail into 'em as we did into Beantoe and Spider that time."

"Sure," agreed his brothers.

"Come on, Freshies! Open up or we'll break in!" and the summons was a thundering one.

"Coming!" cried Pete gaily, and he swung back the portal to confront a crowd of Sophs and Juniors, who had taken it unto themselves to do some hazing.

"Oh, this is fruit! This is easy!" was the cry, as they saw the Smith brothers.

"Please—please you—you won't be too—too rough, will you fellows?" pleaded Pete, in simulated terror.

"Rough? Oh no, we'll be as gentle as lambs; eh boys?" retorted one of the hazers.

"Oh, no, we won't do a thing to them!" cried another.

"Who's in the next room?" demanded the leader of the band.

"Bondy Guilder," replied Bill, indicating the room adjoining his, where the wealthy lad was domiciled.

"And on the other side?"

"Whistle-Breeches Anderson."

"Good! Yank 'em both out, boys," was the order, and some of the cohorts left to execute it, while our three heroes were pulled and hauled from their apartments, going not unwillingly, as they thought of Cap's plan.

"Out on the diamond with them," ordered the leader, who was addressed as "Senator" but with whom the Smith boys were not acquainted. "Bring along the other two."

Pete and his brothers soon found themselves in the midst of a motley crowd of Freshmen, more or less alarmed over the ordeal in prospect. Some were cravenly begging to be let off. Others were threatening and some, like our friends, were silent, taking it as a matter of course.

"Now then, the gauntlet for some one," ordered the Senator. "Line up, fellows. Here's a good one to start with," and he hauled Bondy Guilder out from the press.

"Hands off!" exclaimed the wealthy lad angrily.

"Oh, ho! High and Mighty; eh? Well, that doesn't go at Westfield. Send him down the line, fellows," and the Senator gave Bondy a shove. The hazers had lined up in two files, armed with bladders, rolls of papers, books and stockings filled with flour. It was a reproduction of the old Indian gauntlet along which hapless prisoners had to pass, being beaten and clubbed as they ran.

"You chaps are doing this at your own risk!" cried Bondy trying to break away.

"That's all right, sport! We'll chance it," came the answer. "Run, you lobster, or you'll get the worst of it!"

"I—I protest!" cried the victim, as he turned to see who had hit him with an inflated bladder, in which corn rattled.

"He doth protest too much!" cried a laughing hazer, fetching Bondy a resounding thump with a slap-stick.

"Run!" shouted the Senator, giving him another shove, and the wealthy lad ran perforce, since he was half-pushed, half-pulled the length of the double line.

And what a trouncing he got! He was at once recognized as a supercilious and overbearing lad and the punishment to fit the crime was duly meted out to him. He reached the end of the gauntlet rather much the worse for wear, and his spruce new suit was in need of a tailor's services.

"Now for the next!" cried the Senator. "Where's that Whistle-Breeches fellow?"

"Here," answered Anderson.

"Well, we'll let you off easy, for you look like a good sort." Whistle-Breeches was grinning in an agony of apprehension. "Can you sing?" he was asked.

"A—a little."

"Dance?"

"Even less."

"Good, then you'll do the Highland fling. Here, who's got the mouth organ?"

"I have," was the answer from the ranks of the hazers.

"Pipe up a Scotch hornpipe. Where's that whitewash brush, and skirt. Off with his trousers."

Before Donald could protest he was minus his lower garments and a short skirt of Scotch plaid had been slipped over his head, and fastened behind. Then a dangling whitewash brush was hung about his hips, in imitation of a Scottish costume, and while the mouth organ made doleful music Whistle-Breeches as well as he was able, which was not very good, did a dance.

"Livelier!" was the command, amid a gale of laughter, and livelier it was, until even the hazers were satisfied.

"Next," called the Senator, like a barber.

"Here are three we can work off together," volunteered some one, and Pete, Bill and John Smith were thrust forward.

"What'll it be?" demanded the Senator.

"Blanket tossing," called several.

"No, the pond test."

"Too cold for the water. We'll give 'em the blanket degree. Bring out the woolens."

Some heavy horse blankets were produced and with the hazers holding to the corners, our heroes were tossed up into the air, and caught as they came down with sickenish feelings. But they had been through the ordeal before, and knew what to do. They kept quiet and were not hurt.

But when Bill and Pete were tossed together, it was not so much fun, and they very nearly had an accident. Altogether it was rather a tame hazing, and the Sophs and Juniors felt it so.

"The pond! The pond!" was the cry.

"That means a ducking," said Cap in a whisper to his brothers. "We won't stand for that. Let 'em take you along easy, until they get you right to the edge, and then take a brace, and pitch in the first man you can grab. I'll whistle when it's time. They won't suspect anything."

"The pond! The pond!" was the cry again raised, and though the Senator and some of the older students were a bit averse to it they had to give in to the majority.

"Come on!" cried the crowd, hustling Pete and the two other lads along. "It'll be over in a minute and you'll feel better for it," consoled one hazer to Cap.

"Do you really think so?" he asked gently.

"Sure," was the reply, and the youth wondered why the three did not make more of a fuss. He found out a little later.

"Much against our will, we are compelled to initiate you into the mysteries of the Knights of the Frogs," said the Senator, as the crowd lined up on the bank of a pond not far from the football gridiron.

"Go ahead," said Cap easily, glancing on either side where his brothers stood. "Is it deep?"

"Only to your waist," answered the Senator. "Can you swim?" and he was in earnest for he would have stopped the hazing had he found either of the candidates deficient in the watery pastime.

"A little," admitted Bill. "Oh, please—please don't throw us in!" he pleaded suddenly.

"No, don't—I—I have a cold," added Pete, taking his cue.

"I—I'd a good deal rather have something else, if it's all the same to you," put in Cap, pretending to shiver.

"I thought we'd get their goat!" shouted a lad who had been disappointed that the candidates did not show more fear. "All ready now, in with 'em!"

The three Smith brothers allowed themselves to be led close to the edge of the pond. On either side of each lad stood a hazer, with one hand on a collar and the other grasping the seat of the trousers.

"All ready!" again called the leader. "I'll count three and in they go!"

"One!" came the tally, and the throwers swayed their victims slowly to and fro.

"Two!" came the count.

But before the third signal could be given there came a whistle from Cap. At that instant the hazers had eased back ready for the forward motion at the word three!

But it did not come. Instead Pete, Cap and Bill seemed to slip down. In an instant they were loose. But they did not run.

Instead they put out their feet, one after the other gave vigorous shoves, and six forms, dextrously tripped, lay prostrate on the sod. They were the forms of the lads who had expected to toss into the pond the three Freshmen.

"In with 'em!" cried Cap, and before the astonished hazers knew what was up, one after the other had been rolled down the sloping bank of the pond, into the water.

The tables had been turned most effectively, and, as our heroes fled off through the night they heard some one call:

"For the love of tripe, what are we up against? Who were those fellows?"

"Th—those—those Smith boys!" was the spluttering answer of one who crawled out of the frog pond.

CHAPTER VII

MOVING THE SENIOR STONE

"It occurs to me," remarked Cap Smith one evening about a week after the hazing, when his two brothers and Whistle-Breeches had foregathered in the elder Smith lad's room for a talk, "it occurs to me, fellows, that we're not doing much to uphold the honor and dignity of the Freshman class. What about it?"

"Not doing much?" demanded Bill. "Say, didn't we put it all over the fellows who tried to haze us?"

"Yes, for the time being, but they caught us later, and man-handled us about twice as badly as if we'd let them carry out the original program," answered Cap musingly.

"Well, didn't we win the cane rush, and can't we carry our sticks?" asked Pete as he mended a broken bat in anticipation of spring.

"Yes," admitted Cap, "we did win the rush, and we ought to have, for the Freshman class is big this term. That's what I'm complaining of, it's so big, and there are such a lot of fine fellows in it—not to mention ourselves—that it ought to do something to make its name known and feared for generations to come in the annals of Westfield."

"Meaning just what?" asked Whistle-Breeches, as he carefully marked a page in his algebra, lest he forget it.

"Meaning that we ought to get busy. Now have you fellows anything to propose?"

"We might paint the class numerals on the bell tower. That hasn't been done in a couple of years I understand," spoke Bill.

"Childish," was Cap's objection.

"Let's go about town, changing all the signs in front of the stores," came from Pete. "The Freshmen did that one year, and a chap with a pair of shoes to fix took them into a millinery joint. That would be sport."

"Regular high-school game," was what Cap said. "That's old. Think of something new."

"Besides, it isn't altogether safe," added Whistle-Breeches. "I tried to get some signs for my room the other day, and I did get a nice one from a ladies' hair dressing parlor, but the proprietor turned out to be a man, and he spotted me. It cost me just seven-fifty for that sign. I could have had one made for a dollar. I'm not stuck on the sign racket. But, Cap, how about taking down the Junior flag pole? We could dig it up some dark night and shift it over to the football field."

"That wouldn't be so bad," remarked Cap condescendingly. "But I have what I think is a better plan. You know that big meteor, or piece of a meteor, that stands just off the middle of the main campus?"

"The Senior stone?" asked Bill.

"That's it. Now what's the matter with taking that and depositing it on the college front steps some dark night?"

"What, move the Senior stone?" cried Whistle-Breeches aghast.

"Exactly," answered Cap, "it isn't chained down; is it?"

"No, but it weighs several tons," declared Bill, "and besides it is almost sacred. Why, it's a piece of a meteor that some polar discoverer brought back and presented to the school. The Seniors have always claimed it, and that's where they hold their farewell doings every commencement."

"I know it," said Cap. "All the more reason for moving it. The meteor must be tired of staying so long in one place. Besides we owe the Seniors something, for the way they turned in and helped the Juniors haze us this term."

"But—move the Senior stone!" gasped Pete, as if it was a crime unheard of.

Those Smith Boys on the Diamond

The Senior's stone at Westfield was an ancient and honorable institution. I forgot how many years it had occupied a spot on the campus, and, as Bill said, the graduates always gathered about it at Commencement and had "doings" there. The stone, which was of meteoric origin, was very heavy, and was considered almost sacred to the upper class. Freshmen were required by school tradition to take off their hats when passing it.

"Now what do you say to it?" asked Cap, when the idea had sufficiently filtered through the minds of his brothers and their visitor. "Wouldn't that be worth doing?"

"If we could manage it," answered Pete. "But it's infernally heavy, and how could we shift it?"

"Easy," answered Cap. "I've got it all worked out."

"It would take half the class to carry it," went on Bill, "and if we get a crowd like that out on the campus at night the faculty would be on in a minute, to say nothing of the Seniors."

"I don't intend that half the Freshman class, or even ten members of it shall have a part in it," went on Cap. "We four are enough."

"What, to move that big stone?" cried Bill.

"Hush!" exclaimed his elder brother. "Do you want to give the scheme away? Not so loud. Evidently you haven't studied physics lately; and the principles of the wedge, lever, pulleys and the like are lost on you. I have the very machine needed to move the stone, and if you fellows will help we can do it to-night."

"Of course we'll help!" said Pete.

"We haven't done much lately," added Whistle-Breeches. "I'm with you. But why to-night? It's late now."

"So much the better. We can get out without any one seeing us. Besides the Seniors are having a class meeting to-night and they won't spot us. If you're ready come on."

The others hesitated a moment, and then prepared to follow Cap. That leader, having ascertained by a careful observation that the coast was clear below, let himself out into the corridor, went down it a short distance to see that no scouting monitor was on the alert, and then signalled to his brothers and Whistle-Breeches.

A little later four shadowy forms, skirting along in the darkness made their way softly out of the school grounds.

"Where are you going?" asked Bill, as Cap led them along a road which was dug up for the putting in of a sewer and water system. "This is as bad as crossing the Alps."

"Well, beyond the Alps lies Italy, and beyond these dirt piles is the machine we need for moving the Senior stone, my lads," was Cap's whispered answer. "Come on, we are almost there."

They proceeded in silence until there came a sudden cry of dismay from Bill.

"What's the matter?" inquired Cap.

"Oh, I stumbled in a hole! Say, it's as dark as red ink, and full of gullies along here."

"You're as bad as Beantoe," declared Pete. "Come on. How much farther, Cap?"

"It's around here somewhere I think. I spotted it to-day as I was coming from town, and that's how I happened to think of the scheme. Ah, here it is," and in the semi-darkness he went over to something that looked like half of a wagon truck. It consisted of two high wheels, with an iron arrangement between them, a long pole or lever and several chains.

"What's that, for the love of tripe?" demanded Bill.

"That," said Cap, "is a stone-carrier, a pipe-carrier, a stump-puller and is also used in a variety of other ways to lift heavy weights and transport them from one place to another. The technical name has escaped me, but I think that will answer you," and with this delivered in his best class room style, Cap took hold of the long pole and began moving the machine out from amid a pile of sewer and water pipes.

"Say, I believe that *will* do the trick!" exclaimed Bill admiringly.

"Of course it will," declared Cap. "Come on, now. We haven't any too much time, for the Seniors may come out of meeting any minute, and some may take a notion to stroll around the campus, though it's not likely."

Behold the conspirators then, a little later, trundling the big two-wheeled affair along the dark road. Fortunately the dirt was thick, and the machine made no noise. Also the campus grass was long and soft and the wheels rolled smoothly along.

A careful bit of scout-work on the part of Bill, a cautious approach and soon the plotters were beside the meteor ready to fasten the chains around it, lift the heavy weight by the enormous leverage of the long handle, and wheel it to the main school steps.

Cap and Bill adjusted the chains, handling them with care, so that they would not rattle. The links were soon fastened about the stone.

"All ready now?" asked Cap in a whisper, as he took his place at the lever.

"Let her go," answered Pete.

Cap and his two brothers bore down on the handle. Something began to give. Suddenly there was a hoarsely whispered appeal.

"Oh! For cats' sake! You've got my foot caught in the chains! You're lifting me with the rock!"

It was the unfortunate Whistle-Breeches who had been stationed near the meteor to steady it when it was raised from its ancient bed.

"Hurry up, get loose!" commanded Cap, and he and the others raised the pole until the chains were slackened sufficiently for Donald to get his foot out.

"All right, go ahead!" he called.

There was a creaking of wood and metal. The big lever came slowly down. More slowly Whistle-Breeches saw the meteor being raised. At last it was free from the ground, and was slung, in the chains, between the two big wheels.

"All right!" he whispered. "She's free!"

"Come on then," ordered Cap, and they started across the campus, pulling after them the Senior stone, which from the time when the mind of man ran not to the contrary, had reposed in a place of honor. Now it was moved.

"Right in the middle of the steps," suggested Cap, and they bent their course in that direction. A little later the heavy stone, weighing several tons, was carefully lowered on the big paving flag that marked the beginning of the main school entrance.

"I rather guess they'll open their eyes when they see that," said Cap, as he wheeled the machine away, and stood off to observe the effect. Truly the meteor rested in a strange place.

"Come on—no time for artistic observation," suggested Bill. "We may get caught. Let's make a get-away."

"Sure," agreed Whistle-Breeches, and silently through the darkness they sped with the wheeled affair.

As they were leaving the college grounds they heard some one approaching along the road which they must take to return the lifter.

"Some one's coming! Duck!" whispered Cap hoarsely.

"And leave this?" asked Bill.

"Sure. Shove it into the bushes."

They tried to carry out this plan, but, even as they were doing so some one came into sight. There was just light enough to see that the man was Professor Landmore of the science class, and at the sight of him the four lads, abandoning the machine, made a headlong dive for the bushes.

"Who's there?" demanded the professor, suddenly halting.

No answer, of course; only the sound of hurried flight.

"I demand to know if you are Westfield lads!" went on the instructor vigorously.

"Think he recognized us?" asked Bill, as they paused for breath, for they were now well hidden.

"I don't think so," answered Cap, peering through the bushes.

"He's gone to look at the two wheels," reported Bill, who was also making an observation.

"Then we're safe," decided Cap. "He'll make a book of notes about it, and calculate how much more weight it could lift if it had bigger wheels, and a lever twice as long. Come on, we'll get back to our little beds," and he started away as stealthily as possible.

"But won't he see the machine, and know how the stone was moved?" asked Pete.

"What of it? We can't help it, and even a member of the Senior class in differential calculus and strength of material will know that meteor couldn't move of itself. As long as Prof. didn't see us I don't care. Come on."

And, before they made their silent ways into their rooms that night, the four conspirators took another look at the big stone of Senior fame, resting in its unaccustomed place.

"There'll be a row in the morning," was Cap's opinion.

CHAPTER VIII

ORGANIZING THE NINE

NOBODY was late for chapel next day—a most unusual occurrence. But the news of the removal of the stone had early become known, and before the first call for breakfast almost the entire school was out on the campus, gazing at the work of the Smith boys and Whistle-Breeches.

"Say, that was a peach of a stunt all right," was the general comment. "Who did it?"

"Well, if we find out who of you Freshies did it, there'll be something *else* doing," was the angry retort of the Seniors, since, just before leaving the stone, Cap had painted on it in hastily scrawled characters:

"COMPLIMENTS OF THE FRESHMEN."

"Don't you wish you knew?" demanded Pete, with a wink at his brothers.

"What would you do if you did know?" asked Bill.

"Make you fellows roll it back with your noses," was the grim answer.

"How in the mischief did they do it?" some of the cooler-headed Seniors wanted to know.

"Why the little beggars must have used a platform, on long poles to carry it on," decided one of the upper class. "Though how they got away with it, and so quietly, is a mystery. How are we going to get it back?"

"Have to hire a gang of men I guess," said a companion dubiously.

The matter was spoken of by Dr. Burton at the morning exercises, and he requested whoever had perpetrated the "alleged joke," as he called it, to make himself, or themselves, known. Of course no one confessed, nor did the good doctor expect them to, but he had done his duty, and then he hurried back to his study to resume work on translating some clay tablets, of early Assyrian characters, a friend had sent him.

It was Professor Landmore who solved the problem, by telling his class that day of a curious machine he had seen for applying the principle of the lever, and he described the big two wheeled affair he had noticed beside the road the previous evening. Then the secret was out, and the Seniors learned how the trick had been worked. It was even rumored that the Smith boys had had a hand in it, but nothing came of it, and the upper classmen had to endure the taunts and stings of the Freshmen until, by hiring some of the sewer contractor's men, the stone was put back in its old place.

But the joke created quite a stir, and our heroes were considered "honor men" in the Freshman class, which had gained undying fame by so simple a means, for it was many years before the story of the removal of the Senior stone grew stale in the annals of Westfield.

But now matters were more or less settled down in the school, and our three friends gave at least part of their time to study. Meanwhile they had joined several Greek letter fraternities, and were having their share of college life. They wanted to make the Varsity football team, but failed, as there was an overabundance of material that fall. However they did make the Freshman team, and proved themselves worthy of the honor. But as I intend to tell of the prowess of the Smith boys on the gridiron in a book to follow this, I will merely mention now that Bill, Pete and Cap did more than their share of work in winning the Freshman championship for the school, after many hard-fought battles.

The final game on the gridiron had been played, and the Westfield Varsity had won. Long hair was sacrificed to the barber's shears, dirty suits and leather pads were laid away, and nose guards and helmets put upon the shelf until another fall. Then began a winter of more or less discontent, according as the lads liked or disliked study. Our heroes were about the average, neither better nor worse.

There was rather a more balmy feeling to the air than had been noticed in some time. The snow had gone, and the grass that had been brown and sear was beginning to take on a tinge of green. Cap Smith, mending a rip in his big catching mitt looked out of the window, yawned and stretched lazily.

"Too much study?" asked Bill.

"No, I think I'm getting the spring fever. How about you, Pete?"

"Same here. I'm tired of this measly Latin. Say, where is that new mushroom bat I bought the other day?"

"I don't know, unless Whistle-Breeches borrowed it to prop his window up with. Jove! but it's getting warm!"

"I like his nerve if he has," and Pete made a hasty journey to the room of the lad at the end of the corridor, returning with the stick in question, and followed by the culprit himself.

"I didn't know it was a *new* bat," said Whistle-Breeches in extenuation. "Besides there won't be any baseball for a month."

"There won't, eh?" retorted Bill. "I'll bet they'll have the cage up in the gym this week."

"I heard something about it," admitted Cap. "Mr. Windam, the coach, said he'd soon be on the lookout for candidates."

"Think we have any show?" asked Pete eagerly.

"I guess so. We had a good record from home."

"That doesn't count so much here," was the opinion of Whistle-Breeches. "I'd like to make the nine, but I'm afraid I won't."

"Where do you play?" asked Cap, sizing up his chum with a professional eye.

"Right field."

"Then you bat some?"

"I did a little better than two eighty-nine last year," was the modest answer.

"Then you ought to get in all right. Now I want to catch, and Bill wants to pitch," went on Cap, "and—"

"And I'd like to fill it at short," interrupted Pete.

"And that's the trouble," came from Bill. "It would look too much like a family affair if we were all on the nine."

"Oh, I don't know," said Whistle-Breeches. "If they want good players—"

"They'll take us," declared Cap with a laugh. "Well, even if we can't make the Varsity, we'll have some games. I wish the ground would dry up a bit, so we could get out and have some practice."

Bill leaned forward and looked from the window, which gave a view of a path leading to the gymnasium. On a post not far away from the building was a bulletin board, and at that moment Forbes Graydon, captain of the Varsity nine, was tacking something up on it.

"Wonder what that is?" asked Bill idly.

"Let's go look," proposed Pete. "Come on, Whistle-Breeches."

They hurried down, and after a hasty reading of the placard waved their hands to Cap and Bill, who soon joined them, together with a throng of other students.

For the notice gave announcement that all who wished to try for the baseball team were to report in the Gymnasium that afternoon, when matters pertaining to the organization of the nine would be talked over.

"Shall we go, fellows?" asked Cap.

"Go? You couldn't keep me back if you hitched me to the Seniors' meteorite," declared Bill with energy.

"Going to try for it, Bondy?" asked Whistle-Breeches of their wealthy neighbor at Bill's end of the corridor.

"Me? No. Baseball is such a rough and dirty game. But I shall cheer for our team, and back it with my money, of course. Do you think we have a chance to win the championship? I'd like to wager something on it."

"Oh, you and your money!" growled Whistle-Breeches as he turned away in disgust. "We play ball at Westfield for the *game*—not for *bets*!"

"Ah—really!" exclaimed James Guilder in supercilious tones as he wiped his glasses with his silk handkerchief.

There was a big crowd in the gymnasium that afternoon, when Mr. Windam, who occupied the platform with Captain Graydon and J. Evans Green, the manager, banged his gavel for order.

"You all know why we are here, so there is no use wasting time going over that," said Mr. Windam. "There are several vacancies on the Varsity nine, and we shall be glad to have new candidates announce themselves. You new men will all be given a fair try-out, and those who do not make the team will become substitutes.

"I might add, though you probably all know it, that we won the pennant last year by only a narrow margin. It is going to be hard to keep it this year, for I understand Tuckerton College, our most formidable rival, has an exceptionally strong team, and they are after our scalps."

"Well, they won't get 'em!" Voice from the throng.

"Not if we can help it," went on the coach. "Only I want to warn you that we expect top-notch playing from every member of the team. Financially we are in good shape, and just as soon as the candidates can be picked out we'll begin work in the cage. This week, if possible.

"Now, Mr. Green, Captain Graydon and myself will take your names if you will come forward."

There was a moment's hesitation, and then Cap Smith, with a look at his two brothers, arose and walked toward the platform. There was a murmur in the throng as Pete and Bill followed, and as Whistle-Breeches got up.

"The whole Smith family!" called a voice, and there was a snicker of mirth.

"Well, maybe we'll be glad of more of the Smith boys before the season is over," said Mr. Windam good-naturedly. "Now boys, your names, and the positions you'd like to have."

The organization of the Westfield nine was under way, and as Cap and his brothers noted the number of candidates they began to fear that their chance of all being together on the team was a slim one.

CHAPTER IX

BILL IS HIT

"WELL," asked Mr. Windam, as Cap stood before him. "What name?"

"Smith—John."

"Um. Spell it with a 'Y'"

"Not much. Just plain Smith."

"Good; and the position?"

"Catcher."

"We've got three, but never mind. Accidents will happen. Next!"

"Smith," said Bill laconically. "Plain Bill."

"I see. And you'd like to be—"

"Pitcher."

"Good again, as Mr. Pumblechook would say. Do you know Mr. Pumblechook?"

"Slightly," answered Bill, as he recalled his Dickens.

"Pitcher; eh?" mused the coach, as he jotted Bill's name down. "We've got about seven candidates, but the more the merrier. Glass arms are catching. Next!"

"Smith—Peter," and the third member of the well-known family stood forth.

"Great Scott! Any more? What is this anyhow, a family affair?"

There was a laugh, and Mr. Windam wrote Pete's name down with "shortstop" opposite it.

"Not so bad," the coach murmured. "We need a good man at short, and you look as if you'd fill the bill."

Sawed-off smiled in a gratified manner, and the taking of names proceeded. There was a large number of candidates, and they appeared promising, the coach, captain and manager agreed as they looked them over later. Then, announcing that work in the cage would start in two days, and admonishing the lads to be on hand, and do their best, the meeting was called to a close.

"Think we'll make it?" asked Bill anxiously as he and his brothers, together with Whistle-Breeches, walked to their rooms, to at least make a pretense of reading and studying.

"We will if work is going to count for anything," declared Cap.

The work soon began, and within the next few days there was a considerable weeding-out.

Our heroes were lucky, or, rather their former good playing stood them in excellent stead, and they, together with their friend of the former corduroy trousers, were among the fit survivors. True they were not assured of any particular positions on the team, but they realized that they would be fortunate if they made the Varsity at all. In batting Pete did better than either of his brothers, and he received some compliments from the coach.

Cap was on the anxious seat regarding his position behind the bat, and it was not until on one occasion he did some fearless work, and demonstrated a good throwing ability that he drew from the coach and captain a word of praise that meant much.

"I guess you'll do, 'Plain' Smith," said the coach with a reassuring smile. "Of course I can't tell until I see you out of doors, but you look good to me."

"How about Bill?" asked Cap anxiously, for he wanted to see his brother fill the twirling box, and he knew that the control Bill had of the ball, his curving ability, and his lasting qualities would win him a place if he had a fair try-out.

"Well, I don't know," was the somewhat dubious answer. "Alex Mersfeld pitched all last season, and naturally he's entitled to it again. He's our star man, but of course if your brother is better—well, we've got to have the best—that's all. I don't play any favorites."

And with this Cap had to be content.

Spring came with a rush, the ground dried up, and two weeks after the applications for the team were all in out-of-door practice was ordered. Then the ranks were further thinned, but our heroes and Whistle-Breeches still held their own.

Cap was slated as first substitute catcher, and Pete was honored with a firm place on the Varsity as shortstop. But with Bill it was different. Mersfeld held his old position, and there was no denying that he had a good arm.

Still, when Bill got a chance to show what he could do he opened the eyes of the coach and captain.

"If we ever need to take Mersfeld out there's a chap who can fill the box to perfection," declared Mr. Windam. "I almost wish we could play him regularly."

"But he's only a Fresh," objected the captain, "and if we put the three Smith boys on the team, it'll be said we are trying to make a family affair of it."

"Can't help it—we want to win."

And, as the days went on the Smith boys further demonstrated their abilities. Practice was now held regularly and there were games between the Varsity and scrub nines, Bill pitching on the latter team. His curves were a source of wonder and delight to his team mates, and chagrin to his opponents, and on one occasion, when they did not get a hit off him in five innings, the coach shook his head in doubt.

"I don't know about it," he murmured. "If he keeps on improving as he has he'll displace Mersfeld."

Those Smith Boys on the Diamond

"Nonsense!" said the captain easily.

It was one afternoon toward the close of a practice game, when the scrub was one run ahead, and the coach was exhorting the Varsity lads to "perk up," and put some ginger into the contest. Bill was in the box, and had been doing some excellent work for the scrub when Graydon, of the Varsity, came up to the bat.

"Now's a chance to strike me out!" he called good-naturedly. "If you don't I'm going to make a home run."

"Then you'd better go sit down now," replied Bill, as he wound up for a swift out. It went from his hand with a speedy whizz, and the batter caught it squarely on his stick. There was a resounding whack, and the ball came straight for Bill, at about the level of his head.

He put up his hands for it, instinctively, but so swift was the horsehide sphere traveling that it broke through and hit him on the head, just over the left eye. He dropped like a stone, and Graydon, tossing aside his bat, raced for the fallen lad.

"By Jove old man!" he cried contritely, all thoughts of the game forgotten. "I'm sorry for that. Wow! But that's a nasty bump!"

Poor Bill was lying in Graydon's arms, unconscious, while a big lump was swelling up on the pitcher's head.

"Some water!" cried Graydon, and they brought the pail. Pete and Cap hastened up, as did Mr. Windam.

"Now don't cut off all the air," said the coach. "Harris, perhaps you'd better ask Dr. Blasdell to step down," there being a physician on the school's staff of teachers.

But Bill opened his eyes as the cold water trickled down his face, and murmured:

"I'm—I'm all right. I'm not hurt—just a little dizzy."

"Take it easy, old man," advised the coach. "A little more water. Here, Snyder, mix a little of that aromatic spirits of ammonia. You'll find the bottle in my valise," for Mr. Windam kept a few simple remedies in readiness for first aid to the injured.

Soon Bill was much better, and there was no need for the services of Dr. Blasdell, who came hurrying down at the summons. He found that there was no apparent injury to Bill's skull, and the plucky pitcher wanted to go on with the game, but they would not hear of it, and put another man in, while our hero was taken to his room to lie down. The Varsity won the game, but took little credit for it, and when the contest was over there were many inquiries for Bill.

"Well, how do you feel?" asked Pete the next day, as his brother got up and looked in the glass at the strip of plaster over the big bump, for the skin was broken.

"I feel as though I tried to stop a taxicab with my head. Dizzy, you know. But I guess it will pass over."

He felt much better as the day passed, and wanted to get into practice that afternoon, but the coach would not let him.

However, on the following afternoon, Bill insisted so strenuously that he was allowed to get into a uniform, and take his place on the diamond. There was no game, but he and Cap did some work together.

The first few balls Bill pitched went a bit wild, and his brother did not pay much attention to them, but when, after he had delivered about the seventh one, and it went wide of the plate, Cap called:

"Get 'em over, Bill. They're a bit too far out."

"Too wide! What's the matter? That cut off as big a corner of the plate as you'd want."

"What? It was four inches out."

"Nonsense!" exclaimed Bill. "You can't see straight. Here, how's this?"

The ball shot from his hand, but Bill had to step some distance out to gather it into his big mitt.

"Worser and worser," he said with a smile. "Guess your vacation didn't do you any good."

"Say, what's the matter?" demanded Bill somewhat peevishly. "I'm getting those over all right."

"Then there's something the matter with your eyes," declared his brother seriously, and he looked anxiously at the younger lad.

"Watch this!" called Bill.

He threw very carefully but he seemed to lose control of the ball, which ability was one of his best features. It again went wide, and Cap had to reach out for the sphere.

The catcher shook his head.

"How are your eyes, Bill?" he asked kindly, walking toward his brother. "Maybe the jar they got when you were hit, sort of put them on the blink for a few days. Don't you think so?"

"I don't see how it could be. Just try a few more."

They did, but Cap only shook his head. Other players were noticing something wrong, and as soon as Cap saw this he called the practice off.

"We've had enough for to-day," he declared, as though it was of no consequence, but Bill knew that his brother's light tone covered a deeper meaning. There was a vague alarm in the heart of the lad who aspired to be the Varsity pitcher.

Was his eyesight going back on him? Was he losing his control? What ailed him?

He hardly dared answer, yet he resolved to put it to the test soon.

"My head does feel a little queer," he admitted to himself, and much against his will. "And my eyes—my eyes—I wonder if there can be anything wrong?" and he walked moodily off the diamond, while Cap and Pete gazed apprehensively after him.

CHAPTER X

THE DOCTOR'S VERDICT

"Maybe if you take a few days' rest you'll be all right, Bill," suggested Pete a little later, when the brothers were in their connecting rooms.

"That's it," agreed Cap eagerly. "A rest will do you good, Bill, and then you'll be in shape for the try-out just before the first league game. Take a good rest."

"I'm not tired," protested Bill who sat in a corner nervously fingering his pitching glove. "Why should I need a rest?" He asked the question fiercely as though there was some disgrace attached to it.

"But your eyes," said Cap. "You know you're off in your pitching."

"That's right—I did rotten to-day, and if I'd been in a game they'd have knocked me out of the box. But I'll be all right in a few days more. That lump is still as sore as the mischief," and he tenderly felt of the place where the batted ball had hit him.

"And if you don't get all right?" asked Cap softly.

"Then I'll see a doctor!" exclaimed Bill with energy. "I'm not going to lose a chance to pitch on the Varsity this season, and I believe I will have a chance. I've been watching Mersfeld, and he's not such a wonder."

"I don't think anything of him," admitted Cap. "I've caught for him in a couple of practice games, and he hasn't half your speed, though he has some nice curves, and a good control. I don't believe he'd last through a hard game."

"Oh, we'll fix Bill up, and have him on the Varsity yet," declared Pete easily. He could afford to speak thus for he was sure of his own position at short, and Cap had at least a tentative promise of being behind the bat in a number of the big games that would soon be played.

The brothers talked over the situation, and then fell to studying, with more or less energy, until interrupted by the entrance of Whistle-Breeches and Dick, or "Roundy," Lawson, the genial senior having gotten into the habit lately of calling on his neighbors.

"What's wrong?" demanded Whistle-Breeches as he noticed Bill's rather dejected attitude.

"Oh, I'm on the blink. Can't see to throw straight," and then the story, which was already known to several in the school, was told.

"I'll tell you what it is," began Lawson, and his words were carefully listened to, as befitted a Senior. "You want to see a doctor, Bill."

"You mean Doc. Blasdell?"

"No, he's all right for a pain on your insides, but I mean an eye doctor—an oculist. I know a good one. I had trouble with my eyes once, and I went to him. He can fix you up. Maybe there's a little strain which some medicine will cure. Why don't you go to see him?"

"I believe I will. It's tough to be knocked out before the season starts. I'll go to-morrow."

Then they fell to talking of the baseball prospects, how this player was making out at first, another in the field, what the chances were for good batters, the prospects of Westfield holding the pennant, and kindred matters.

All the while Bill sat in a darkened corner, for Lawson had insisted on this since his advent into the room, saying that darkness was good for weak eyes. And poor Bill fingered his pitching glove, wondering if he would ever get back into the box again. Cap was straightening a bent wire in his mask and Pete was re-winding some tape on a favorite bat that always opened at the split every time he used it. But he could not bring himself to throw it away.

"Mind now," stipulated Lawson, as he and Whistle-Breeches took their leave, "you see that eye man to-morrow."

And Bill promised.

They went to the oculist's together, Cap and Bill, and the pitcher was put through a number of tests. He sat and looked at candles, while the medical man put a lens in front of the lights, and turned the glass sideways to make the single image develop into two. Then when Bill admitted that the two lights were not on the same level (as they should have been to one of normal vision) the oculist shook his head doubtfully.

Next he looked through the eye away into the back of Bill's head, with a queerly constructed instrument, and reflected glaring lights into the lad's orbs until he blinked in pain. Reading cards of different size type, taking a stick, and trying to impale a series of concentric circles, first with his left eye closed and then with the right one shut, ended the test.

"Well," announced the oculist at length, "it's not as bad as it might be. Your left eye is considerably out of focus, and I should say it was caused by some pressure on the optic nerve—possibly the result of that blow with the ball."

"But what can be done about it?" demanded Bill with a note of despair in his voice.

"Well, nothing much. In time it may readjust itself, and again—it may not."

"Do you mean that I'll always be this way—not able to throw straight?" demanded the pitcher almost springing up from his chair.

"Easy now, old man," cautioned Cap in a low voice.

"Won't I ever be able to throw straight again?" cried poor Bill.

"I'm afraid not," answered the doctor. "Of course if the pressure on the nerve could be removed it would be possible, but that would take an operation, and I don't recommend it. In fact it might make matters worse. But it's not so bad. It will cause you no annoyance."

Those Smith Boys on the Diamond

"No annoyance?"

"Not a bit. You can see as well as ever. You can read, write, walk about, in fact only in matters requiring a critical judge of distance will you be at all hampered."

"But that's just it!" cried Bill. "I *need* to be a judge of distance if I'm going to pitch on the team."

"I'm sorry, but you can't pitch any more," was the doctor's verdict, and to Bill, who like his brothers had his whole soul wrapped up in baseball, the words sounded like a doom.

"Not pitch any more?" repeated Bill dully.

"Not until that nerve pressure is removed," was the answer, "and I advise against any operation for that. I can fit you with a pair of glasses that will take off any strain when you are reading, and that's all you need. But you can't pitch—that is if you have to be accurate."

"And that's just what I have to be," murmured Bill. "Not pitch any more—not pitch any more," and he covered his eyes with his hand, and swayed uncertainly.

"There—there old man!" spoke Cap, a trifle hoarsely, for he was much affected by the way his brother had taken the blow that had fallen. "Maybe it won't be as bad as it seems. You may get better."

Bill shook his head despondently.

"Come on," he said to his brother. "I—I'll come back for the reading glasses later, doctor. I—I don't just feel like it now," and Cap linked his arm in that of Bill's and led him away, the footsteps seeming to recite mockingly over and over again, like some death knell.

"You can't—pitch—any—more! You can't—pitch—any—more!"

CHAPTER XI

MEETING AN OLD FRIEND

For some time after leaving the doctor's office neither Cap nor Bill spoke. The latter stumbled along, his mind filled with gloomy thoughts, and as for Cap he was wondering what he could say to take the pain from his brother's heart. Wisely he concluded that he could say nothing. At length Bill spoke.

"Well, what do you think of it?" he asked.

"It might be worse," replied Cap, as cheerfully as he could.

"Worse!" Bill laughed mirthlessly. "I don't see it."

"Why you might be blind, or not able to see to read or get about without wearing goggles and using a cane. As it is you only needed specs to read with. And maybe the nerve will get well of itself."

"Yes, after the season is over, and I lose all chance of playing on the Varsity. I tell you I want to pitch, Cap. That's one reason why we picked out Westfield,—because of the good nines they have here."

"I know it; but what's to be done? If you can't control the balls, and place them where they ought to be, you know—"

"Yes, I know how it is," and he spoke bitterly. "I'd be of no use in the box. Well, I s'pose there's no help for it," and Bill picked up a round stone, and threw it at a telegraph pole. He missed it by a foot, though usually he was a good shot. He laughed mirthlessly, and turning to Cap said: "See how it is?"

"Oh, well, don't take it so hard. That was a nasty blow you got, and the effects may be a long time wearing away. But I'm sure you'll be all right next season, if you're not this."

"But a whole season off the diamond!" gasped Bill in dismay.

"Oh, you don't need to get off. Maybe Windam will play you in the outfield. You can catch; can't you?"

"Yes, but I want to be in the box. However if I can't—I can't," and seeing that he was causing Cap pain by his manner, Bill tried to assume a more cheerful air.

"Graydon will be cut up over it," said the elder lad, referring to the player whose batted ball had been responsible for Bill's mishap.

"It wasn't his fault," declared the pitcher. "I ought to have known better than to try to stop it at such close range. It was going like a bullet. I should have passed it."

"You couldn't—and be a Smith boy," exclaimed Cap with a laugh. "We'd take a chance on anything in the shape of a ball, I guess."

"Well, I'll go back in a couple of days, and get the reading glasses, and maybe they'll help some," decided Bill, as they walked on. They were nearing the college, the many buildings of which could be seen in the distance above the trees, the red tiled roofs making a pretty picture seen through the green foliage.

"Hello, something's going on!" exclaimed Cap, as they swung into the main road that led up to the grounds. "Look at the crowd."

"Baseball game?" suggested Bill.

"No, they're away this side of the diamond. There's some sort of a wagon there—a Gypsy van, I guess. Maybe some of the fellows are having their fortunes told. Come on, we'll get in the game, and have some fun."

"Maybe it's an ambulance, and some one is hurt."

"Get out! They don't have ambulances around here."

The brothers increased their pace, and as they neared the vehicle something vaguely familiar about it attracted the attention of Bill and Cap. They looked at each other.

"It can't be him!" exclaimed Bill.

"It looks like his rig, though," assented Cap. "But it's painted a different color. I wonder—?"

"Hark!" cautioned his brother.

They were close to the throng of students now, but could only see the top of the wagon, which was a covered one. A voice could be heard droning away like this:

"Young gentlemen, it is one of the greatest pleasures of my life to speak to students—to persons of learning, in which class I am so fortunate as to count myself, though in an humble capacity. Learning, I may say, extends even to the noble steed which draws my equipage, whose cognomen is, I may say derived from—"

"That's all right, old sport, what's the horse called?" demanded one of the students, with a laugh.

"Yes, get down to business," added another.

"Right you are, young gentlemen," admitted the voice, though Bill and Cap could not yet see the speaker. They observed their brother Pete beckoning frantically to them, and they increased their pace. "Right you are," resumed the owner of the covered wagon. "The name of my noble animal is Pactolus, called after, I need not remind you—"

"The river of Lydia in which the King Midas washed himself one Saturday night, so that he put the golden touch on everything," interrupted one of the classical students, and there was a laugh, but it did not disconcert the traveling vendor, for such Bill and Cap now knew him to be.

"Exactly," he admitted. "The river whence ever after the visit of the king, the sands became golden. Thus I named my horse Pactolus in the hope that some day he might stumble into a river which, if it did not turn him to gold might at least make him a steed of silver.

"But, young gentlemen of Westfield, which I understand is the name of the school in the distance, I did not attract you hither by the magic of my voice and playing to talk to you on classical subjects. This is a practical world, and we who live in it must also be practical. Whoa, there, Pactolus!" This as his steed showed signs of restiveness, due to the fact that some of the boys were tickling his ears.

"Whoa, Pactolus. Never mind if some of your longer-eared brothers are whispering to you to entice you away to pastures green—stay you here!"

This reference to donkeys had the effect of causing the mischief loving lads to hastily draw away from the horse, in some confusion, for there were snickers at their expense.

"It is a practical world," resumed the speaker, "and we must recognize that, and be practical ourselves. Now there is nothing more practical for the removal of any kind of misery, whether inward or outward, than my Peerless Permanent Pain Preventative, which is good for both man and beast, and eradicates all the ills that flesh is heir to, and some that it is not. Good for man and beast I repeat. See! I use it on myself," and suiting the action to the word, the man, who had black flowing locks, as Bill and Cap could now see, and who wore light trousers, a red and green striped vest and a red shirt with black polka dots—this man vigorously rubbed some stuff from a bottle on his big forearm.

"There I had a pain—'twas there, 'tis gone. 'Twas mine, 'tis yours—for the asking," and he waved his hand toward the throng of students who laughed again, and seemed amused by the clatter of the traveling medicine man.

"Think not it is only for external pain—'tis also for the ills of the inner organs. See, I take some thusly," and, tilting back his head the speaker swallowed a generous potion from the bottle. "Good for man and beast," he went on, smacking his lips. "As harmless as a baby, and as powerful as an electric current. See, Pactolus minds it not, yet it will take the stiffness from him like magic," and, leaning forward he rubbed some of the contents of the bottle on the animal's flank.

Pactolus merely looked around, waved his ears slowly to and fro, and seemed to take but a mild interest in the matter under discussion. Probably he was used to it.

"Now who wants a bottle of this wonderful remedy?" went on the man. "The regular price is one dollar, but to introduce it among gentlemen of learning I am selling it for the small sum of twenty-five cents—a quarter—and it would be cheap at half the price. Or, if you have no immediate need for this, let me introduce to your favorable consideration and notice, my Rapid Robust Resolute Resolvent, which is a cake of soap guaranteed to take out stains on linen, silk, wool, cotton, velvet, calico and satin, the skin of the hands or face, from wall paper, newspaper, writing paper or wrapping paper. Positively nothing like it known to science.

"Or, if you care not for these, I have others. My Spotless Saponifier is a soap worthy to be used by all the gods that on Olympus dwell, and it sells for only ten cents a cake. An' you like that not, let me introduce to your polite and favorable consideration my Supremely Sterling Silver Shiner. Nothing like it known for cleaning silver, gold, brass, copper, pewter, iron, lead, bell-metal, watch chains, baseball bats, and gloves, and for brightening up a dull intellect it has no equal, though I despair of selling any for that purpose when I gaze on the bright, smiling and intelligent faces before me."

There was a mocking groan from the students at this, and some more laughter.

"And now," went on the vendor, "who will be the first to purchase some of my Peerless Permanent Pain Preventative, my Rapid Robust Resolute Resolvent, my Spotless Saponifier or the Supremely Sterling Silver Shiner? Who will be the first?" and the man, who was as gaudily attired as his wagon was painted, advanced into the crowd.

There was a moment of hesitation, and then Cap, Bill and Pete, who were standing together, exchanging queer glances, heard Bondy Guilder say in a low voice to some of his particular cronies in the sporting set:

"I say, fellows, let's have some fun. Let's upset his old apple cart, and spill his Pain Killer and other stuff. He has nerve, trying to do business so near the school. There ought to be a rule to keep these peddlers away. Let's make a rough house for him."

"Sure! Go ahead! We're with you!" agreed several. "Come on, we'll all make a rush together."

Those Smith Boys on the Diamond

Cap and his brothers heard. They looked at each other and nodded.

"Here you are, young gentlemen! Here you are!" the voice of the vendor was murmuring. "You have listened with gratifying attention to the patter of Professor Theophilus Clatter, and now you may buy his wares. You need not beware of the wares of Theophilus Clatter!" he declaimed in a sing-song voice.

"That's him!" exclaimed Pete.

"Of course," agreed Bill.

"And they're going to make a rough house for him," added Cap. "Shall we stand for it?" he asked in a low voice.

"How are we going to stop them?" demanded Bill.

"If we say he's a friend of ours I think they'll pass it up."

"Acknowledge him as our friend before this crowd — tell how we traveled with him and sold patent medicines," asked Pete. "They'd laugh at us!"

"What of it?" inquired Cap indignantly. "Professor Clatter helped us when we were in a hole, after we'd run away from home. It's up to us to help him now. I'm going to stand up for him. If the boys get going they'll demolish the wagon, and everything in it. We can't have that."

"I guess not," agreed Pete and Bill in low tones.

"Come on then," suggested their elder brother, edging his way through the throng.

The plan proposed by the rich bully had taken the fancy of his fellows. The word was passed around and the students got ready for a rush that would overturn the wagon. Already they were jostling the professor who was aware of a change in the temper of the students. He looked around uneasily, and glanced back at his wagon. Quite a throng was now between him and the vehicle. He turned to retreat, vaguely alarmed, but found himself cut off.

Those Smith Boys on the Diamond

"My Rapid Robust Resolute Resolvent," he was saying, "is guaranteed to—"

"Come on now, fellows, over with the wagon!" cried Guilder. "Altogether, with a rush! Make a rough house! This faker has no business here!"

The rush started but before it could get under way, Cap, Pete and Bill Smith had sprung up on the steps that were let down from the back of the vehicle. They stood together looking over the crowd of their fellow students.

"Hold on!" cried Cap calmly, raising his hand for silence.

"What's up?" demanded Bondy with a sneer.

Professor Clatter, with a look of wonder on his face was staring at the three Smith boys.

"No rough house here," said Cap determinedly, noting with relief that nearly every one in the crowd was a Freshman. Had they been Sophomores, Juniors or Seniors he would hardly have dared take the stand he did.

"No rough house? Why not?" demanded the rich lad. "Why can't we have some fun with this fellow?"

"Because," went on Cap resolutely, and no one knew what an effort it was to make the announcement in an exclusive crowd of students, "this man is a friend of my brothers and myself. If you're going to make trouble for him, you've got to reckon on us," and Cap standing there, with his brothers beside him, looked sturdy enough to put up a pretty good argument.

"Your friend?" sneered Bondy.

"Our friend," repeated Cap calmly. "So you'll please pass him up, as a matter of class courtesy."

It was an appeal that could not well be denied.

"Listen to Professor Clatter's friend!" cried several of Bondy's cronies.

"Proud to acknowledge it," put in Bill in drawling tones, "and so would you, if you knew the story."

Professor Clatter was still staring at the three lads on the steps of his wagon.

"The Smith boys! The Smith boys!" he murmured. "I'd never have believed it. Whoa, Pactolus! We have unexpected allies," and he made his way through the crowd of wondering students to where our three heroes waited for him on the wagon steps.

CHAPTER XII

PROFESSOR CLATTER'S PLAN

STANDING there, facing their fellow students who were gathered in a mocking crowd about the medicine wagon, Cap, Bill and Pete hardly knew how to begin, nor what to talk about after they had started.

"Do you mean to say you're going to stick up for—for *this* person?" demanded Bondy, and he put all the scorn of which he was capable into the words.

"We certainly do," declared Cap firmly. "If you'll let us explain, we'll—"

"Young gentlemen, permit me," broke in the voice of Professor Clatter. "I believe I can—"

"No more of your patent medicine jargon!" interrupted some of Guilder's cronies. "We've had enough."

"I wasn't going to speak of my wares," said the vendor simply. "I hope you will give me credit for knowing how to deal with gentlemen—when I see them."

There was a laugh at this, and the Professor knew he had at least some of his audience with him.

"I was going to ask my friends, the Smith boys, to allow me to make the explanation," Mr. Clatter went on. "I believe I can give all the facts necessary."

He looked at Cap, who nodded an assent. Then, mounting the steps beside the lads, the vendor of the Peerless Permanent Pain Preventative and the various other nostrums, told simply, but effectively, how, one morning, he had met our three heroes as they were fleeing from home, under the mistaken notion that they were to be tarred and feathered. Mr. Clatter related how he had provided them with breakfast from his wagon, how they had traveled about with him, selling his goods, taking part in a sort of minstrel show, all as related in the first volume of this series.

"And when I was arrested for innocently practicing palmistry, in an effort to locate a man who had robbed their father, these boys kept on with the business alone, and made money enough to pay my fine," said the professor. "I can never thank them enough for what they did, and now they have more than ever put me in their debt by standing up in this friendly fashion for me when—well, I know you young gentlemen love fun, but this wagon and stock is all I have in the world," he concluded simply, and there was a break in his voice.

For a moment there was silence, and then the story, which the professor told much more dramatically than either of our heroes could have presented it, had its effect.

"By Jove! That was no end of a lark!" exclaimed Roundy Lawson. "I wish I could travel around like that, and eat when I pleased."

"That was *rich*!" declared Whistle-Breeches Anderson. "Why didn't you ever tell us that, Cap?" he demanded.

"I never thought you fellows would care about hearing it. But now, boys, do you blame us for sticking up for Mr. Clatter?"

"Not a bit of it!" came in an emphatic chorus. "You're all right, professor!"

"Pass out some of that Rapid Resolute Resolvent!"

"I want some of that Spotless Soap!"

"Me for the Pain Killer. I ate too much dinner!"

"A little silver polish will about suit me!"

The students were clamoring for the wares, now, and the vendor, who had shaken hands with our heroes, and whispered to them how grateful he was, began passing out his goods. Whether the students really wanted it, or only bought out of sympathy, or because of a class spirit, mattered little as long as he sold the articles, and the professor did a thriving trade.

Those Smith Boys on the Diamond

"Come on," disgustedly called the rich lad to the cronies in his own particular set, "I might have known better than to come to Westfield. I was warned that a number of common persons attended it, and now I'm sure of it. I shall write father and have him withdraw me at once."

"Why don't you withdraw yourself, and save daddy the trouble?" asked Whistle-Breeches as the rich lad passed on amid his chums, with a sneer on his face.

All danger to the professor's wagon was now over, and he at once made friends among the students, for he was a man who had traveled much, and his ways, while suiting his particular business, were genial and kindly when once you knew him, though at first they might seem bombastic and uncultured. He knew how to gain the attention of an audience.

"Well, it's a real pleasure to see you boys again," went on the professor when the desire of the crowd for his wares had been satisfied, and when most of the students had strolled away. "And so you are attending school here? Well, what has happened since last we met?"

"Lots," declared Cap, and he proceeded to tell the main facts.

"Are you still traveling about in the same way?" asked Pete.

"Yes, but I don't do any more palmistry. It's too risky. But what's the matter with you, Bill? You don't seem well."

"Got hit with a ball," explained the lad, touching the place where there was still a lump on his head.

"Too bad, but you'll soon be over it. Pactolus once kicked me, and it was a week before the swelling went down."

"The swelling is the least part of it," spoke Bill gloomily, and Pete, who had not yet heard of the result of the visit to the oculist, looked in alarm at his brother's tone.

"What's the trouble?" inquired Mr. Clatter. "Perhaps some of my pain killer will help you. It's good stuff in spite of the way I sell it. I used to know something of medicine. Let me wrap you up a bottle for old times' sake."

"No," answered Bill wearily, "it isn't the pain. But I can't pitch any more," and he told the whole story, sitting inside the wagon, which was equipped for living in Gypsy fashion, his brothers and the professor listening sympathetically.

"Can't pitch; eh?" murmured Pete. "That's tough."

"It sure is," declared Bill. "And I've got to wear glasses when I read. I might as well resign from the team right away."

Professor Clatter looked critically at the lad who sat near him. Though it had been many years since the vendor had played ball, he had not lost his love for the game, though he never belonged to a regular nine. But he appreciated what it meant to Bill.

"When do you get your reading glasses?" he asked casually.

"Oh, I'm in no hurry to become a 'four-eyes,'" replied Bill bitterly. "I'll get them next week. Jove, but it's tough!" and he shook his head.

"Well, we must be getting back," said Cap, after a pause. "I've got some boning to do."

"Same here," added Pete. But Bill got up in silence to follow his brothers.

"Can't you come and see me again?" asked Professor Clatter anxiously as his young friends descended the steps. "I'm going to stay in this neighborhood for some days and I'd like to talk over old times with you. Yes, Pactolus, I'm going to unharness you, and let you crop of the green herbage," and he proceeded to release the horse from the shafts. "Pactolus and I understand each other," he went on. "At least he knows what I say to him, though I have not yet mastered his language. It takes Dean Swift for that."

"Has he stumbled into the river of gold yet?" asked Cap.

"Not yet, but I look at every stream eagerly as we pass over or through it, when it is not too deep. Some day perhaps the sands will

Those Smith Boys on the Diamond

be golden," and the medicine man laughed gaily. "But do come out and see me some night when you have a chance. I'm going to camp on the other side of town. Come out to-night, if you will. I'll probably have an old friend there to greet you."

"Who?" asked Pete. "Not the thumbless man?"

"No, he's safe in jail, I hope. But what would you say to Duodecimo Donaldby?"

"The weather prophet?" asked Bill, with a show of interest.

"The same," answered the professor, "though whether he is still engaged in making it rain, or whether he is doctoring horses I know not. He changes his occupation from day to day, and from night to night, like the phases of the moon, but I expect him."

"Then we'll come," decided Cap earnestly. "I should like to see him again. Dear old Duodecimo! He was a queer chap."

"And he hasn't changed any," was the professor's opinion. "Well, I shall expect you then. Remember, on the other side of town. Now can't I give you some soap, or pain killer or—or something?"

He seemed so eager about it that they did accept a bottle of the pain killer, which was excellent for sprains. Then they took their leave, promising to come back that night.

"I expect to do a little business early in the evening so if I am clattering when you arrive, just wait in the crowd for me. I still do some singing and banjo playing to draw a throng. I don't s'pose you boys would like a try at your old job?" and he laughed heartily.

"I'm afraid it would hardly be in keeping with our characters as students at Westfield," said Pete. "But say, if you'll stay around here long enough maybe we can get the glee club to do a stunt for you."

"That would be asking too much," declared the genial professor, with a wave of his fat hand on which still sparkled the diamond ring. "Well, farewell until the shades of night do fall."

Those Smith Boys on the Diamond

"The same old professor," remarked Cap, as he and his brothers strolled toward the school buildings.

"Yes, I'm glad we could help him—they would have put him on the blink for keeps," said Pete earnestly if a bit slangily.

Bill said nothing, but there were bitter thoughts in his heart as he walked on, and nothing his brothers could say or do served to cheer him.

Meanwhile Professor Clatter, standing in the back room of his wagon, which was his house, his store, his sleeping apartment and his theatre of entertainment, watched the three boys.

"Fine fellows," he murmured. "It's too bad about Bill. I wonder if I couldn't help him? He'll have to wear glasses—wear glasses and play ball—I wonder if it could be done? I don't see why not, especially in the pitcher's box. Now I wonder if Duodecimo will be on hand?

"If he comes I have a plan to propose to him! Jove, I don't see why it wouldn't work. If he hasn't forgotten all he used to know about eyes it ought to! I'll chance it, anyhow. Yes, that's what I'll do. Maybe I can fix up a scheme so that Bill can pitch on the Varsity team after all. I'd like to. Yes, I'll propose it to Duodecimo, and see what he says," and, filled with pleasant anticipations about his plan, Professor Clatter proceeded to get his simple meal on the little oil stove he carried in his wagon.

"What ho! Mercurio!" he cried, clapping his hands. "Come, base varlet, set out the magic table, for I am an hungered and would'st dine!"

And then, having given his orders to his menial, Mr. Clatter, highly pleased, proceeded to carry them out himself.

CHAPTER XIII

BILL IS HIMSELF AGAIN

"WELL, are you coming?" asked Pete of Bill as he tossed into a corner of his study one of a pile of books over which he had been doing more or less "boning" in the last hour.

"Coming where?"

"Over to see Professor Clatter. Cap's ready."

"Oh—I don't know." Bill spoke listlessly. He had been trying to study but a curious watery mist came into his eyes, and, try as he did to brush it away, the film seemed to return. The eye near the injured spot smarted and burned.

"Come ahead," urged Cap, entering his brother's room at that moment. "Whistle-Breeches wants to go and see the performance."

"All right, you fellows go, and I'll stay here. I don't care much about it."

Cap winked at Pete. They understood Bill's despondency, and were determined to get him out of the slough of it.

"Oh, it'll be sport—like old times," urged Cap. "The professor will do his singing and banjo act, and I've a good notion to get up on the platform and show Whistle-Breeches how we used to earn our board and lodging."

"Better not, Bondy might spot us and there'd be a faculty row. He'd be just mean enough to squeal. But come on, Bill. The professor expects us. Say, remember the time after he got nabbed, and we tried to take the spot out of the man's vest, and it turned green, red, yellow and a few other colors? Remember that, Cap?"

"I should say I did!" exclaimed John Smith. "I thought sure it was all up with us," and he laughed heartily. A smile came over Bill's gloomy face. Pete saw it and nudged his brother.

"We'll see the rain-maker again," went on Pete. "Better come, Bill. Don't worry about your eyes, and pitching and all that. Maybe it will come out right."

"Yes, it's easy enough for you fellows to talk, for you can play ball, but—Oh well, what's the use of kicking. I s'pose I'll get in form again for next year," and with rather a bitter laugh Bill prepared to follow his brothers.

As they had been on their good behavior of late, and as there was such a competition for places on the ball team, it was decided that they should get permission to make a trip to the village instead of trying to run the guard.

"I'm not hankering to have the proctor's scouts nab me," explained Cap, "and I guess we can get a pass all right if we put it up to Nibsy good and strong," the aforesaid proctor who rejoiced in the appelation Alexander McNibb being thus designated.

They obtained permission easily, though the proctor looked at them rather sharply, and Pete wondered if he recognized in him and his brothers the lads who had, a few nights previous, wheeled a town sprinkling cart into the middle of the school inner court and left it there with an admonition printed on a big placard adorning it, recommending that certain members of the sporting crowd get aboard the water vehicle. But if the proctor knew anything he kept it to himself, and, a little later the three Smith boys, and Whistle-Breeches were trudging toward town.

They saw the glare of the gasoline torches on the professor's wagon before they heard his voice, but it was not long ere they recognized his resonant tones calling out the merits of his Rapid Robust Resolute Resolvent and other wares.

There was a large throng about the wagon, and business was good. The professor, looking over the heads of his audience recognized our heroes, and nodded to them pleasantly, yet never ceasing his "patter." Between the sale of his remedies and soap, he rendered several ballads accompanying himself on the banjo.

"It sure does remind me of old times!" exclaimed Pete, humming the chorus of the song the professor was singing.

"Cut it out!" advised Cap hastily.

Bill was not very talkative, but Whistle-Breeches enjoyed the affair immensely, and was greatly interested in what Professor Clatter called his "patter."

"We ought to get him to some of our class rackets," said Donald. "He'd be no end of a lark."

"I guess he doesn't stay in this part of the country long—nor, in fact anywhere more than a couple of nights," replied Pete, and, as he spoke he looked beyond the gaudily decorated vehicle of the medicine vendor and caught a glimpse of another wagon drawn alongside the road. It was one with something like a three inch quick-firing gun projecting from the covered top, and Pete whispered to his brothers:

"There's Duodecimo Donaldby's rig if I've got my eyesight left. I wonder if he's shooting rain-making bombs for a living now, or curing sick horses?"

"We'll soon know," said Cap. "The professor is nearly through."

The crowd having exhausted the entertaining features of the medicine man's little effort, and the sale of the remedies and soaps being about at an end, Mr. Clatter announced that he was through for the evening. The people began to disperse, and soon Cap, with his two brothers and Whistle-Breeches were seated inside the snug little wagon, enjoying a cup of tea and some cakes which the professor set before them.

"I'm glad you boys came," he said, as he looked in the tiny teapot to see how much of the beverage remained. "I want to have a talk with you—but hold on, I was almost forgetting an old friend."

He stepped to the window of his vehicle, poked out his head, and gave a call which was at once answered. Presently some one was heard approaching, and, as the door opened the head of the character known to our friends as the "rain-maker," was thrust inside.

"Welcome to the Smith boys!" he called.

"Enter!" invited Mr. Clatter.

"Yes, come in and talk over old times, Mr. Donaldby," added Pete.

"Hush! Not that name!" exclaimed the weather prophet, with a warning finger laid athwart his lips. "Not that name or by a shattered cirrus-nimbus cloud you'll have the authorities about my ears!"

"How about Mirthrandes Hendershot?" asked Cap.

"No—no! Not that! Not that! Spavin, ring bone and blind staggers are things of the past. I dare not undertake to cure any more horses."

"Just what *are* you doing?" asked Pete, as the former weather prophet entered and took a low stool.

"Ah, now we are coming to it," was the answer with a smile. "In the first place my name—how does Tithonus Somnus strike you?"

"An odd combination," remarked Cap, recalling the one ancient god who was turned into a grasshopper, and the other who symbolized sleep.

"Odd, and so much the better," went on Mr. Somnus. "It typifies my calling."

"Which might be—?" asked Bill suggestively.

"Which might be almost anything, and nothing, and which, at times is neither or both, but which at present is that of astronomer ordinary. That is my present occupation. I go about the country initiating the farmers and country folk into the mysteries of the heavens. In fact I jump about from place to place, hence the name Tithonus. I jump while others sleep, and show the stars which only come out at slumber-time—hence the name, Somnus. Is it clear?"

"Perfectly so," answered Whistle-Breeches, who thought the astronomer a most delightful character.

"And so you are showing the stars and moon?" asked Pete.

"On all except cloudy nights," was the reply. "I find it pays well. Only misfortune seems to follow me. The other night when there was a most delightful moon, I had trained my telescope on it, and was admitting the populace to the view at so much per 'pop' as it were. I could not understand the murmurs of indignation that arose from some of the gazers, nor the expressions of wonder from others, until taking a look myself, I saw a strange and weird countenance peering at me from the end of the telescope. I had been describing the mountains of the moon, but lo! they turned out to be the whiskers and eyes of my pet cat Scratch, who, perched upon the roof of my wagon, was calmly gazing down through the object lens."

"A cat!" cried Cap. "No wonder the people couldn't understand what they saw."

"And so I was in ill-repute," continued the astronomer gloomily, "and had to travel on. Then it was cloudy to-night so I can do no trade. But enough of this, tell me of yourselves," which the boys proceeded to do.

The talk worked around to Bill's misfortune, and as soon as this topic was reached Professor Clatter, who had hitherto been talking but little, evidenced a sudden interest.

"Now it is my turn to say something," he said. "I asked you boys to come here for a purpose, and the purpose was connected with my friend Duodecimo—I beg your pardon, Tithonus Somnus. In the first place, Tithy, which I will call you for short, in the first place, Tithy, have you forgotten what you used to know about spectacles?"

"Spectacles? No," was the reply. "But what in the world has that to do with baseball, and the fact that Bill will have to give up pitching?"

"I'll get to that in time," replied the professor. "You used to go about the country fitting people with glasses, did you not, Tithy?"

Those Smith Boys on the Diamond

"I did, until they passed a law requiring one to maintain a fixed residence if he would practice as an oculist, and then I became a weather prophet, a rain-maker, a horse doctor and other professional men in turn."

"Exactly," said the professor. "And am I right in thinking that you still have your eye-testing apparatus with you, and also some of the spectacle lens?"

"You are. In fact I have made a small telescope of some of my glasses. You may not think so," he went on, turning to the lads, "but I received a fine medical education, and I specialized in eyes. I was once considered a good oculist, but love of a roving life precluded me practicing with success. Still I have not forgotten my knowledge."

"I thought not!" exclaimed Mr. Clatter with energy. "That's why I asked the boys to come here to-night to meet you. I had a plan in mind, and I hope, with your aid, Tithy, to carry it out.

"Bill, here, wants to pitch on the Varsity nine. He has a good chance, or, rather he had a good chance, until his unfortunate injury lost him a certain necessary control of the ball. Am I not right?" he asked, appealing to the youth in question.

"That's right," answered Bill, wondering what was going to happen.

"Very well then. Now it seems that with the proper glasses the temporary defect in your vision would be corrected as far as reading was concerned; wouldn't it?"

"That's what the doctor said."

"Correct again. Now then, if you can wear glasses to read with, why can't you wear them to play ball with?"

"Play ball in glasses!" cried Bill.

"It has been done," went on the professor easily. "Of course it would be rather hard for a catcher or a baseman to wear them, with the necessity of having to catch balls thrown with great swiftness. But it's different with a pitcher. He practically only throws the ball, and it is returned to him easily. Glasses would not be a hindrance to you. In fact, in your case, they would be a help."

"I—I never thought of wearing glasses and pitching," stammered Bill.

"All the more reason for thinking of it now. Here is my plan."

The professor motioned for the boys and the astronomer to give close attention.

"We'll get Tithy here to give you a good examination," said Mr. Clatter, "and we'll have him make you a special pair of glasses. He'll put them in a strong frame, so they will set close to your face, and fasten on securely. They won't come off no matter how hard you run, and in fact you may not need them when you're at the bat. But you do need them to pitch with, and you're going to have them. Can you make an examination to-night, Tithy?"

"Better than in daylight. I have all the instruments, and I think I could make the glasses."

"Then it's all settled!" declared Mr. Clatter, as if that was all there was to it. "Come along, boys, we'll go over to the other palace car, and see what happens. Bill, you're going to pitch again, and if you don't make the Varsity it's your own fault!"

The medicine man had rattled on at such a rate that the boys had hardly had a chance to speak. As for Bill his brain was in a whirl. He did not know whether or not to have any faith in what was proposed.

"Do you really think it can be done?" he asked.

"Of course it can!" declared Mr. Clatter.

"I can make the glasses all right," answered Mr. Somnus with professional pride.

"But could I pitch with them on?" asked Bill.

"I don't see why not," was Cap's opinion.

"Wouldn't the fellows laugh me off the diamond?"

"I'd like to see them do it!" exclaimed Whistle-Breeches fiercely.

"If you can't play, after you show that you can still pitch as good as before, Cap and I won't be on the team," declared Pete with energy.

"Oh, I'm not going to act that way about it," spoke Bill, but there was a more hopeful look on his face.

A little later he was again being put through the eyesight test. Mr. Somnus, as he preferred to be called, was in his element. He had a very good set of instruments, and he very soon demonstrated that he knew his business.

"Ha! Hum!" he exclaimed from time to time, as he made test after test, and jotted down the results of some calculations on paper. "I find that you will have to have a very peculiar pair of lens," he said. "I haven't them, but I can get them for you."

"And will the defect in my eyes be corrected?" asked Bill eagerly.

"You'll never know you had it," was the confident answer. "The injury was a peculiar one, involving, as the other doctor told you, one of the optic nerves. It may pass away at any time, but while it exists it must be corrected. Glasses will do it, and inside of a week I predict that you will pitch as well as before. Shall I make the glasses?"

"Yes!" fairly shouted Bill. "I don't care what they cost."

The details were soon arranged. Mr. Somnus knew of an establishment where lens for glasses were ground, and he undertook to procure them for Bill. He would return with them in a few days, he said, and adjust them in a proper frame—a frame that would admit of rough play.

"Then we'll see what happens," said Professor Clatter. "I have to travel on in the morning, but I'm coming back to see the test. I'm interested in this," and the honest, if somewhat eccentric character, clapped Bill heartily on the back.

The pitcher's spirits had come back to him, and on the way back to the school that night he laughed and joked with his brothers as before.

It seemed as if the time would never pass. Baseball practice was the order of the day now, and every afternoon the Westfield diamond was thronged with prospective members of the Varsity nine. Cap was more than ever assured of a place as catcher, Pete, as I have said, was the regular Shortstop, but poor Bill had to wait, and see his rival, Mersfeld, filling the box.

"But keep up your spunk," Pete told his brother one afternoon, following a grueling practice. "They're not half satisfied with Mersfeld, and if your glasses are any good at all you'll have his place."

"I don't want to put him out," said Bill. "If I only get a chance to play in some of the big games I'll be satisfied."

He refrained from pitching during the time he was waiting, and was excused from some of his studies until he had the reading glasses the town oculist made for him.

Then, one day, came a note from the rain-maker stating that he and his wagon were in their former place, and that the "ball-glasses," as Bill called them, were ready.

"Now for the test!" cried Mr. Somnus, as Bill, his brothers and Whistle-Breeches arrived at the improvised camp early one afternoon. Cap had brought his mask and glove and was to catch for his brother.

"I hope my plan works," murmured Mr. Clatter.

The special lenses which Mr. Somnus had had made were fitted into a strong, black rubber frame, and it set close to Bill's eyes. It gave him an odd appearance, but it was just the thing for playing a game of ball. He had demonstrated that he could bat well without any glasses, so he would only have to be a "four-eyes," as he dubbed himself, in the pitching box.

The glasses were put on. Bill took a ball, and walked off a short distance while Cap donned his mask and mitt.

"Let her go!" he called to his brother, who was "winding up," in his usual fashion. A square stone had been laid down as a plate.

There was an anxious moment among the little knot of spectators. Bill drew back his hand, worked his arm a couple of times, squinted through the glasses, and then with the speed of a miniature projectile, the ball left his grip and sped toward Cap.

"Biff!" That was the ball hitting the big mitt.

"Strike!" yelled Cap. "It was over the plate as clean as a whistle, but it had a curve to it that would fool Hans Wagner himself! Good work, old man!"

"Try another!" called Bill, trying to keep his voice cool.

Once more the ball went over the plate cleanly.

"Strike!" called Cap again.

"Are they all right?" asked Bill.

"Right as a trivet! Oh, Bill, you're yourself again!"

There was a moisture in the pitcher's eyes, but the odd glasses concealed his tears of gratitude.

"Hurrah!" yelled Professor Clatter leaping about like a boy. "Now you'll make the Varsity; eh Tithy?"

"He will! I can read it in the stars!" said the little astronomer, gaily.

CHAPTER XIV

THE TRY-OUT

THAT Bill was delighted to find his former skill had not deserted him goes without saying. It was tempered a bit by the fact that he had to wear glasses, but that could not be helped.

"I wonder how Mr. Windam will take to 'em?" he asked his brothers as they walked back to school together.

"He won't care as long as you can pitch the way you did this afternoon," declared Cap.

"I wonder what Graydon will say?"

"I don't see how he can say anything," came from Whistle-Breeches. "Any captain wants the best pitcher he can get."

"And as for J. Evans Green, he's the kind of a manager who wants to see games won, and keep possession of the pennant," declared Pete. "There won't be any kicking about the glasses, Bill. He'd let you wear hoop-skirts if it made you play better."

But there was objection to Bill when he appeared for practice wearing the odd goggles, though it did not come from coach, captain or manager. It was first voiced by Bondy Guilder, and some of his cronies.

"Why don't you play a lot of men with crutches, and their arms in bandages?" asked the rich youth with a sneer.

"I would if they could do better than some fellows I know who seem to think a ball will bat itself and catch itself," declared the captain with energy, for there had been a slump in practice that day.

It even extended to Mersfeld the crack pitcher who issued passes to a number of men and was hit more times than he liked to count.

"What's the matter with you?" demanded the coach half savagely as the scrub pulled over three runs in succession, and Mersfeld walked another man to first. "Are you dreaming that this is a tennis match, or don't you want to play?"

"Of course I want to play!" was the reply, "only I can't be at top-notch all the while."

"You've got to!" was the curt decision. "If you don't do better than this in the final try-out you'll be a substitute instead of a regular."

"And I suppose 'Foureyes' Smith will have my place?" suggested Mersfeld with a sneer.

"It'll go to the man who does the best work—four eyes or eight eyes—rest assured of that. Now put some ginger into your pitching, if you can!"

Stung by the words of the coach Mersfeld did a little better, and the Varsity saved the game by a narrow margin. But there were many whispers around the school and in the gymnasium that day there were strange rumors of a shake-up in the team, rumors of the strong nines which the Tuckerton Sandrim and Haydon schools had ready to put on the diamond to battle for the pennant in the interscholastic league.

The opening of the season was not far off. Day by day the practice on the Westfield diamond grew harder and more exacting. Bill had gotten back all his former skill, and the little rest seemed to have done him good, for his speed increased, and his curving ability was considered remarkable by his friends. He had gotten used to the glasses which he only wore when in the box, and he hardly noticed them at all.

Mersfeld, too, had taken a brace, and was doing good work, whereat coach and captain were glad.

"I guess he'll make out," said Graydon one night when he and Mr. Windam were talking over matters. "But I'm glad we have Smith to fall back on."

"So am I. Smith may be first pitcher yet. When have you arranged for the try-out game?"

"Day after to-morrow. We'll play Mersfeld four innings on the Varsity and then give Smith a show. That will be the test."

There was so much interest in the try-out that almost as big a crowd assembled on the diamond to witness it as usually was present at a match game. Bill was a trifle nervous for he realized what he was up against, and as for Mersfeld, that pitcher went about with a confident smile on his face.

"Are you going to make it?" his friends asked him.

"Of course I am," he assured them. "I'll pitch against Tuckerton all right Saturday."

For the first league game was to take place then, and it was unofficially announced that the players who made the best records in this, the final try-out would have the honor of representing Westfield on the diamond at the opening of the season.

"Play ball!" called the umpire, and Bill watched his rival take his place in the box. How he longed to be there himself! But he knew his turn would come, and he felt in his pocket to see if his precious glasses were safe. Without them he would be lost, and he wished now that he had had two pairs made for emergencies. He decided he would try to locate the traveling astronomer and get another set.

The game opened up with a snap, and this was maintained right along. Everyone was doing his best, for it was no small honor that was at stake. There was no denying that Mersfeld did well for the first three innings. There was only one hit off him, and in the fourth he struck out two men in quick succession.

Then, whether it was a slump, whether he went stale, or whether it was nervousness due to the fact that he was under close observation did not manifest itself, but the fact remains that, after getting two men out, he grew wild, passed one of the poorest batters, was hit for a three bagger by the next, and when another got up, and knocked a home run, there was pandemonium among the members of the scrub nine.

"What's got into Mersfeld?" was the general inquiry.

Nobody knew, and when the fifth inning opened, with Bill in the box, there was intense excitement. Bill adjusted his glasses and got ready to pitch.

"Now watch Foureyes put 'em over!" sneered Bondy Guilder.

"That'll do!" called Mr. Windam sharply. "This isn't a match game, and there's no need of rattling one of our own men. Save your sarcasm, Guilder, for Tuckerton!"

Bondy muttered something under his breath, and walked over to talk to Mersfeld, who was darkly regarding his rival from the coaching line.

Bill was a bit nervous but as Cap had been sent in to catch the pitcher grew confident as he saw the friendly face of his brother, and caught the well-known signal for an out shoot.

Bill nodded in confirmation, drew back his arm, hesitated a moment, wondered for one wild second whether he was still himself, and could see to make the curve, and then—he threw.

"Strike one!" howled the umpire, and then Bill knew that he *was* himself, and a fierce joy welled up in his heart. He caught the ball Cap tossed back to him, and sent it stinging in again.

"Strike two!" was the reassuring call, and the batter pounded the plate in desperation, for he had not before moved his stick.

He swung viciously at the next one, and—missed it clean.

"That's the boy!"

"Go at 'em!"

"Put some more over like that!"

"Give the next one a teaser!"

Thus Bill's friends encouraged him.

The try-out game went on, growing more fierce as each player struggled to make a record. Bill was a marvel with the ball. But one hit was registered off him during the five innings that he pitched. After the contest there was a consultation among the captain, manager and coach and it was announced to the anxiously waiting ones that Bill Smith would pitch the first five innings of the opening game with Tuckerton, with Mersfeld as second pitcher, while Cap Smith would catch for his brother, and Dean Denby for Mersfeld.

"I told you that's how it would be!" cried Whistle-Breeches clapping Bill on the back with such heartiness that the pitcher's glasses nearly flew off.

"Boy, I'm proud of you!" spoke Cap fervently.

Mersfeld said nothing but there was a bitter feeling in his heart.

"An upstart Freshman!" he muttered as he passed by Bondy Guilder.

"That's what," agreed the rich youth, "and I'd like to see him taken down a peg. Do you know how it can be done?"

"No," replied the rival pitcher.

"Come here and I'll tell you," suggested Bondy, and the two walked across the diamond arm-in-arm, talking earnestly, and the talk boded no good for Bill Smith.

CHAPTER XV

THE CONSPIRATORS

THERE was plenty to talk about that night. The rooms of the Smith boys were thronged with some old and many new admirers, for nothing succeeds like success, and now that Pete was officially named as Varsity shortstop, now that Bill had the preference, at least in the opening game, as pitcher, and when Cap was named to catch for his talented brother our heroes found themselves very much in the lime-light.

"To think of all three of us making the Varsity in our first year!" exclaimed Bill, as he received the congratulations of several new acquaintances.

"It's great!" declared Cap. "I'm afraid our rivals will dub it the 'Smith Nine,' instead of Westfield."

"Let 'em," declared Captain Graydon, who was present. "I don't care what they call the nine if we keep the league pennant. But let me tell you Smith boys, and all you other baseball fellows who are here, it's going to be no easy matter. Tuckerton has a battery that's hard to beat, and Haydon has a better team than ever before. We've got our work cut out for us."

"And we'll make good!" exclaimed Whistle-Breeches, who was happy because he had been promised at least part of the opening game, even though he was in centre field.

But among the visitors to the rooms of our heroes Mersfeld and Bondy were conspicuous by their absence. The failure of Mersfeld to call was commented on, and it was openly said that he was jealous. And as Westfield was an institution where the school spirit was especially strong this was all the more marked.

"I'm sorry there's a feeling between the two pitchers," said Captain Graydon to Mr. Windam as they walked to their dormitories together after the informal little visit. "For both Smith and Mersfeld are fine fellows. We may need them both before the season is over."

"I expect we will. But we couldn't pass over Mersfeld's poor work to-day. By putting Smith ahead of him it may spur him up a bit."

"I hope it doesn't spur him up to any mischief," murmured the captain dubiously.

"Mischief; how?"

"Well, he has a very ugly temper, and once he gets aroused—well, the worst he can do is to withdraw from the team, I suppose."

"I'd be sorry for that," went on the coach. "But we really have a find in Smith. He's better than before his injury, or else those glasses help him."

"I guess it's the glasses. No one's vision is perfect the doctors say, and perhaps we'd all be better for spectacles. I was just thinking what would happen if they became broken in a critical game. Bill couldn't pitch."

"That's so. He ought to have a pair in reserve. I'll speak to him about it."

Then the coach and captain fell to talking about other baseball matters, including the coming game on Saturday, and the chances for winning.

Bill and his brothers rejoiced among themselves, and with their friends, and a letter telling about the honor that had come to the Smith boys was sent to their father, all three joining in making it a sort of composite epistle.

"Two days more and we'll see what we can do on the diamond in a league game," said Cap, as he got ready to do some neglected studying. "Now don't mention ball again for an hour. I nearly slumped in Latin to-day, and if any of us fall behind we'll be hauled up and put out even if we knock a home run. So buckle down, fellows."

Those Smith Boys on the Diamond

It was hard work to apply oneself to lessons after the events of the day, but they did it—somehow.

Meanwhile, strolling along a dark and infrequented road that led back of the school buildings, were two figures deep in conversation.

"It's too risky a game to play," objected Mersfeld, as he strode moodily along.

"But you don't want him to knock you out of your place, do you?" demanded his companion, Bondy Guilder.

"No, of course not. But suppose I'm found out?"

"You won't be. I can get the glasses easily enough, for his room is right next to mine. I was going to change, for I don't fancy the crowd he and his brothers trail in with—they're regular clod-hoppers. I'm glad now I didn't, for it will give us just the chance we want."

"What have *you* got against him?" asked the pitcher.

"Oh, he's a regular muff, and he thinks he's as good as I am," was the illogical answer. "I'd be glad to see him off the nine. It ought to be composed of more representative school fellows, anyhow than a lot of 'Smiths.'"

"I haven't anything against the name, but I have against Bill," said Mersfeld. "He shoved himself in, and pushed me out—and I'd like to get even."

"You can, I tell you. If I get hold of his glasses he can't pitch in the game Saturday."

"Can't he get another pair?"

"Not the way I'll work it."

"Why not? Suppose you do manage to sneak in his room and get his goggles. He'll miss them sure as fate, and send for another pair."

"No he won't."

"Why not?"

"Because I won't take them until Saturday morning, or just before the game, and it will be too late to get another pair. Or, better still, I can take out the special lenses that are in the frames, and substitute others. Then he won't suspect anything, he'll go to the box, pitch so rotten that Graydon will have to take him out, and you'll go in. Bill won't know whether it's the glasses, or whether his eyes have gone back on him again. How's that for a trick?"

"It's all right I guess," was the hesitating answer. "I rather hate to be a party to it," went on the pitcher, who was not a bad chap at heart. "But—"

"But he had no right to come here and supplant you," put in Bondy.

"No, that's right. Well, can you get the glasses from his room?"

"Sure, and I'll arrange to have other lenses to slip in them. I'll get the size, and they're easy to change. I was close to him to-day, and I saw how the rubber frames were made. I guess Bill won't be such a wonderful pitcher when I get through with him," and Bondy chuckled as he and his fellow conspirator turned around and walked back toward school.

CHAPTER XVI

CAUGHT

THERE was an air of subdued excitement all about Westfield, that extended even to good old Dr. Burton. He even found it rather difficult to apply himself to translating some early Assyrian tablets into modern Hebrew as a preliminary to rendering them into ancient Chinese.

The various members of the faculty found their students paying rather less than the usual attention to the lectures, and in one quiz, when Cap Smith was asked concerning the raising of an unknown quantity to the nth power his answer was:

"He's out on first!"

"Doubtless true, but unfortunately Westfield has no chair for the science of applied baseball," answered the professor as the laugh went rippling around the room.

But the spirit of the game was in the air, it hung about the school buildings, lingered in the dormitories, and the very smell of chemicals in the laboratory seemed replaced by the odor of crushed green grass, the whiff of leather and the sound of the explosions of the miniature Prince Rupert's drops, as the science teacher demonstrated the effect of a sudden change in the strain of a congealed body seemed to the lads to be the blows of the bat on a ball.

Over on the diamond, which had been as carefully groomed as a horse before he is led out to try for the blue ribbon, were any number of eager enthusiasts practicing. There were talks between the coach and captain, anxious conferences with the manager, and on every side could be seen lads in their uniforms carefully looking after balls, bats, masks or chest protectors. Some were tightening the laces of their shoes, others mending ripped gloves, while Bill Smith had indulged in the luxury of a new toe plate.

For the next day would mark the opening of the Interscholastic league, and the first big game—that with Tuckerton—was to be played.

"And you must wake and call me early,

Call me early, Peetie dear,

For to-morrow is the opening

Of the dear old baseball year."

Thus Cap misquoted the verse, and joined his brothers and chums in the laugh that followed.

But if there were many hearts that rejoiced at the near prospect of the big opening contest, there were two lads whose souls were filled with bitterness. One was Mersfeld, the partially deposed pitcher, and the other Bondy Guilder, who, for no particular reason, had come to almost hate Bill and his brothers.

"Do you think you can get the glasses?" asked Mersfeld of his crony, on the night before the big game.

"Sure. I've been watching Bill—his room's next to mine you know—and I know just how he goes and comes. I have some ordinary lenses all ready to slip in the place of the special ones I'm going to take out."

"How'd you get the right size?"

"Oh, I made a pretence of wanting to see his glasses and while I had them I pressed a sheet of paper on them, got an impression of the size, and got the lenses in town. They are not an unusual size, only they're ground differently to bring one eye in focus with the other. Bill won't pitch more than one inning in the game to-morrow, and then you can go in."

"But he'll know what's wrong as soon as he has his eyes, and the glasses tested again."

"What of it? He won't suspect us, and all you want is a chance to make good; isn't it?"

"Yes, for if I do make good in the opening game I'm sure they'll have to let me stay through the season, and Bill won't be in it. I'm glad you're helping me."

"I'd do more than that to put one over on the Smith boys. I don't like them. I wish they'd get out of Westfield."

Bondy had his plans all laid, and had, after considerable trouble secured a pair of lenses to replace those in Bill's pitching glasses. Now, like some spider watching for his hapless prey, he sat in his room on the morning of the day of the big game, waiting for a chance to sneak in and make the substitution. He felt that he could do it, for no one ever locked his door at Westfield, and Bill had been in the habit lately of spending a lot of time in the apartment of Whistle-Breeches.

But now Bill was in his room, and Bondy was impatiently waiting for him to go out. The sneak knew that if he could change the glasses the trick would not be discovered until after Bill was in the box, for he did not use the goggles in preliminary practice where there was no home plate over which to throw.

"Hang it all! Why doesn't he go?" thought the rich lad as he peered from the partly-opened door of his study, and saw Bill moving about in his room. The pitcher was taking a few stitches in his jacket, which had been ripped. "I haven't much more time," mused the conspirator, "for they'll soon go out to practice, and he'll take the goggles with him."

There was a call from down the corridor. It came from the room of Whistle-Breeches.

"I say Bill, where are you?"

"Here. What's up?"

"Give us a hand, will you? I can't get this needle threaded and there's a hole in my stocking as big as your fist. I wouldn't mind, only it's opening game and we want to look decent. I caught it on a nail."

"Wait a minute. I'll be with you," sung out Bill, and dropping his own work he darted for the room of his chum.

"Just my chance!" whispered Bondy. "But I haven't much time!" He had the substitute lenses ready, and a small screw driver with which to open the frame and make the change.

Into Bill's room the sneak darted when he saw the pitcher enter the study of Whistle-Breeches. A rapid glance around showed him where the goggles were—in their usual place on top of a shelf of books.

It was the work of a minute to secure them, and begin to loosen the screws. Bondy worked feverishly, but his very haste and nervousness were against him. His hands trembled, and he was in a sweat of fear. One glass was almost loose, when, with a suddenness that was as startling as a clap of thunder would have been, the door leading from Bill's to Pete's room opened, and the shortstop entered. He did not notice Bondy at first, as the latter stood in the shadow of the book shelves, and this fact gave the conspirator time to shove the screw driver and extra lenses into his pocket.

"Caught!" he murmured under his breath.

The tinkle of glass caught Pete's ears, and he wheeled around.

"Oh! Hello, Bondy!" he exclaimed, and then catching sight of his brother's goggles in the other's hands he quickly asked:

"What are you doing with those glasses?"

CHAPTER XVII

BILL'S PITCHING

For a moment Bondy did not answer. On his face there was a sickly grin, and he seemed to turn a sort of greenish white.

"What are you doing with those glasses?" repeated Pete as he took a step forward.

"I—er—I just came in to see Bill," stammered the rich lad. "He was out, and I—I—er I was looking at them. Queer lenses; aren't they? One seems to be loose. I was going to tell Bill he ought to tighten it."

No wonder it was loose, for the sneak had partly taken out the screw. The expression on Pete's face changed. He had had a quick suspicion that all was not right, but he began to feel now that perhaps he was mistaken.

"See, here is the loose glass!" went on Bondy eagerly, for he was quick to notice the altered expression on the other's countenance. "It ought to be tightened, or it might drop out during the game, and become broken. You can tighten it with a knife."

He dared not offer his own screw driver.

"That's right; it does need fixing," admitted Pete. "Much obliged for noticing it, old man. Bill might not have seen it."

"Yes, I just came in—er—to ask Bill how his arm was, and I noticed the glasses," went on the visitor lamely.

"Why, what's the matter with his arm?" asked Pete quickly, and in some alarm.

"Oh, nothing, I—I just wondered if it would hold out."

"Oh, I guess it will. There, the glass is tight now," and Pete, who had used his knife to set the screw, tapped the rubber frame to listen for any vibration. There was none.

"Well, I'll be going," announced Guilder, with an air of relief. "See you at the game. It's most time to start," and he slipped from the room, just before Bill returned.

"I wonder what he wanted?" mused Pete, looking after the retreating figure of the rich lad. "Mighty funny his getting friendly all of a sudden. I wonder what he wanted?"

Pete looked at his brother's glasses. He glanced toward Bondy's room, and pondered again. Just then Bill came in.

"Say, son, you ought to keep these locked up," remarked Pete, handing the glasses to him.

"Why?"

"They might get broken if you leave them around so promiscuous. I just tightened a screw."

"Thanks. Crimps! but I've got to hustle. I was showing Whistle-Breeches how to mend a rip in his stocking. He was for tying a string around it as if it was a bag he was closing up. Well, we'll soon be slaughtering—or slaughtered; eh?"

"Yes, how about you?"

"Fit as a fiddle. I wish I had to pitch the whole game."

"Maybe you won't after you see the way they knock you out. They've got some hard hitters."

"I'm not worrying. Is Cap on the job?"

"Yes, we're all ready. What are you waiting for?"

"Just got to put a few more stitches in this jacket. I'll be right over. Go ahead."

"No, we'll wait for you," and Pete took a chair in his brother's room. He was thinking of Bondy's visit but he made up his mind to say nothing about it at present. After all he might be wrong in his suspicion, but he resolved to keep a sharp lookout.

Those Smith Boys on the Diamond

Soon Bill had finished his sewing task, and went out with his brother. Cap joined them, and a little later they were on the diamond, indulging in some light practice.

Down the road came the sound of songs and cheers, mingled with indiscriminate yells. Then came the blast of horns.

"The cohorts of Tuckerton!" cried Cap. "Here they come!"

Several big stages swung into view, laden down with students and girls, for the boys had brought a lot of their young lady friends to see the game.

The vehicles were gay with colors—flags and banners waved from canes and long staffs. Horns adorned with the hues of Tuckerton were waved and blown. Then came more songs, more cheers, more wild yells, and more rioting of colors, as the banners, flags, ribbons and streamers were shaken at the crowds of Westfield students who poured out and greeted their rivals.

As the stage loads of spectators drew up and were emptied, another carryall swept along the road. It contained the opposing nine, and in grim silence, like gladiators coming to the battle, they alighted.

"Three cheers for the best nine in the league!" called the leader of the Tuckerton cohorts, and the yells came in quick response.

"Now three cheers for the second beet nine—the one we're going to wallop—Westfield!" called the same youth who was almost hidden behind a big bow of his school colors.

Westfield was appropriately serenaded, and then they returned the compliment. The grand stands and bleachers were now beginning to fill, for a game of baseball between these two schools was worth coming a long distance to see.

"Gee! what a lot of pretty girls!" exclaimed Pete as he stood with his brothers near home plate after some sharp warm-up practice.

"You let the girls alone—until after the game," advised Cap.

"There *is* a big crowd," remarked Bill.

"Don't let it fuss you," suggested his older brother, for Bill was likely to get a bit nervous, and he had never played in such a big and important game before. "Come over here and we'll try a few balls. Better wear your glasses to get more used to them."

"Gee! maybe it's a good thing I got caught as I did," mused Bondy as he saw Bill putting on the goggles before the game had started, as he was practicing with Cap. "He'd have found it out by now, and the game would have been all up. But I'll get him yet! I wonder why Mersfeld doesn't come around. He acts afraid."

The other pitcher was afraid—horribly so. His heart misgave him for consenting to the trick, and yet he let it be carried out. At least he supposed it had been, for he took pains to keep out of the way of Bondy. And when he saw Bill in the goggles pitching a few preliminary balls to his brother, he wondered what sort of balls they were.

"How long will he last—how long?" he murmured, for he thought the plot had been carried out.

The crowds increased. The Tuckerton nine and substitutes trotted out for practice, and good snappy practice it was. Captain Graydon shook his head as he watched.

"They'll come pretty near having our numbers," he remarked.

"Nonsense!" exclaimed the coach. "They play fast and snappy, that's a fact, but we can do the same."

"No, that's just where our men fall down," went on Graydon. "They're good stickers, and can pull a game out of the fire in the last few innings, but they don't wake up quickly enough. That's what I'm afraid of. I wish we had decided to let Smith pitch the last half instead of the first innings."

"Say, that's what we'll do!" suddenly exclaimed the coach. "This is the first chance I've had to get a line on the Tuckerton boys, and I believe it will be policy to put Mersfeld in at the opening. He's feeling sore, and he hasn't as good lasting qualities as I'd like. We'll put him up first, and if he can't hold 'em down we can change at any time. I'll tell Smith."

Bill felt a sense of disappointment that he was not to open the game, but he knew better than to dispute with the coach. Cap looked as though he could not quite understand it, and he wondered if it was a sample of what would happen in other games.

"We've got to save you two for a pinch," explained Graydon to the catcher, just before the game was called. "Begin to warm-up again after the third inning."

The preliminaries were over, and the Tuckerton men took their places on the bench, the home team having last chance at the bat. The Westfield nine walked to the field, and Bill and Cap took their places with the other substitutes.

"I wonder what's up?" mused Mersfeld as he was told to go to the box. "He must have the changed glasses and Mindam and Graydon have seen how punk he is even in practice. Here's where I get my chance!"

The game began, and the first crack out of the box netted a two-bagger for the initial hitter of the Tuckerton nine. Mersfeld smiled a sickly smile as the ball came back to him.

"It's all right," called Denby reassuringly from behind the bat. "We'll get this fellow."

Mersfeld did strike him out, after the man had made two foul strikes, and, feeling a trifle nervous the twirler issued walking papers to the next hitter, who had a high average for stick work.

"Work for this man," signalled the catcher to the pitcher, but Mersfeld, as he was about to throw was aware that the first hitter was stealing to third. He shot to the baseman quickly—but wildly. It went over his head, in among a crowd of spectators, and before the ball could be fielded in the man was home with the first run of the game, and with only one out.

Those Smith Boys on the Diamond

What a wild burst of songs and cries of gladness came from the stands where the visitors were! Flags and banners waved, and the shrill voices of the girls seemed to mock the Westfield players.

"Starting in bad," murmured Bill to Cap.

"Oh, well, all our fellows are a trifle nervous. I guess we'll make good."

Mersfeld redeemed himself a few seconds later by striking out the next man up, and with two down, the last man knocked a little pop fly. It looked good but Pete got under it, and had it safely in his hands when the runner was ten feet from first.

"Well, now to see what we can do," remarked Graydon as he came in from first with his men eager to get a chance at the sticks.

They did not do so much, for there was an excellent battery against them, and one run was all they could tally. But it tied the score, and gave the home rooters something to shout for.

Whether it was nervousness or whether his conscience troubled him was not made known, but Mersfeld seemed to get worse as the game progressed. His throws to the basemen were wild, and he practically lost control of the ball, while his curves broke too late, and the opposing team readily got on to them.

"Oh, we've got the pitcher's 'Angora' all right!" chanted the visiting rooters, that being the classical term for "goat" or nerve.

"And I believe they have," admitted the coach, when the fourth inning opened with the score eight to one in favor of Tuckerton. They had garnered two in the second frame, three in the third, and a brace in their half of the fourth. The one lone tally was all Westfield had when they came to bat in the ending of the fourth, and though they worked fiercely not a man got over the rubber.

"Smith and Smith is the new battery for the Westfield team!" announced the umpire as Graydon's men went out to the field at the opening of the fifth. Mersfeld had not said a word when ordered from the box. He knew he had been doing poor work, but with a bitter feeling in his heart he watched to see how Bill would make out with, as he supposed, the changed glasses.

"Now watch the celebrated Smith brothers work!" cried a Tuckerton wag, as Cap and Bill took their places.

"Yes, and they *will* work, too!" murmured Pete.

"At least if we can't get any more runs, I hope we can keep the score down," thought the coach, to whom the game, thus far was a bitter disappointment. All his work so far that season seemed to have gone for naught.

Bill was smiling confidently, as he took his place in the box. The crowd which had not before had a good look at him, caught sight of the goggles, and instantly there was a chorus of cries.

"Foureyes! Foureyes!"

It was what Cap and Pete had feared would happen. Would it bother their brother?

Bill showed no signs of it. He did not appear to resent the name, but smiled back at his tormentors in an easy fashion.

"I wear these so I can strike out more men!" he called.

"I guess he'll do," murmured the anxious captain on first base, and the embittered coach took heart.

Cap and Bill exchanged a few preliminaries, and then signalled for the batter to take his place. The man up was a terrific hitter and Bill used all his wiles on him. First he purposely gave him a ball, and then sent in a slow teaser which the man did not strike at, but which the umpire counted.

"Here's where he fans!" thought Bill, as he tried an up shoot. It made good, and the bat passed under it cleanly. There was a murmur of chagrin from the stick-wielder's fellows and he resolved to knock the cover off the next ball.

But alas for hopes! Once more he swung wildly—and missed.

"Out!" howled the umpire gleefully, for his sympathy was with Westfield, as much as he dared show it.

And when the next two men never even touched the ball there was joy unbounded in the ranks of the home team, for now they saw a chance for victory.

"I don't see that you did anything," whispered Mersfeld to Bondy as the change was made for the ending of the fifth.

"Didn't get the chance," whispered back the plotter. "I was nearly caught. But this isn't the only game. There'll be other opportunities."

Westfield was at the bat, and it must have been the effect of Bill's pitching for every man up made a hit, and the bases were soon filled. But only two runs came in, for the opposing team took a brace at an opportune time for themselves, and in season to prevent too heavy scoring by the Westfield lads.

"Now only six runs to beat 'em!" called Captain Graydon cheerfully, as though that was a mere trifle. "Keep up the good work, Bill, and we'll dedicate a chapel window to you."

Bill did. He surpassed even his own previous pitching records, and did not allow a hit in that inning, while in their half of it Westfield got one, making the score four to eight in their opponents' favor.

"Now for the lucky seventh!" called the coach, when that inning started. "Don't let them get a run, Bill, and help our fellows to pull in about a dozen."

Bill smiled, and—struck out the first two men. Then one of the heavy hitters managed to get under a neat little up shoot, and sent it far out over the left fielder's head. It was good for two bags, and the next man brought the runner in, to the anguish of Bill, who feared he was slumping, as there had been two hits off him in succession. But with a gritting of his teeth he held his nerves in check, and that ended the scoring for the first half of the seventh.

"Now, boys, eat 'em up!" pleaded coach and captain as Bill and his teammates came in. They did, to the extent of three runs, which seemed wonderful in view of what had previously been done, and there was a chance for wild yelling and cheering on the part of the home rooters.

With the score seven to nine, when the eighth opened, it looked better for Westfield's chances, and when she further sweetened her tallies with another run, brought in by Pete, there was more joyful rioting.

"They mustn't get another mark!" stipulated the captain when the final inning opened. "Not a run, Bill."

"Not if I can help it!" the pitcher promised. From a corner Mersfeld watched his successful rival—watched him with envious eyes.

From the grandstand Bondy also watched, and muttered:

"I won't fail next time. I'll spoil your record if it's possible!"

Amid a wild chorus of songs and school cries Bill faced his next opponent. He proved an easy victim, as did the lad following, but from the manner in which the third man began hitting fouls it seemed to argue that he would eventually make a hit. And a hit at this stage might mean anything. For Westfield needed two runs to beat, and they were going to be hard enough to secure—every member of the team knew that.

It was the fourth foul the batter had knocked. The others had been impossible to get, though Cap had tried for them. Now, as he tossed off his mask, and stared wildly up into the air to gage the ball he heard cries of:

"Can't get it! Can't get it!"

"I'm going to!" he thought fiercely. He ran for it, and was aware that he would have to almost run into the grand stand to reach it. The crowd made way for him. Into the stand he crashed, with a shock that jarred him considerably, but—he had the ball in his hands!

"Wow! Wow! Wow!" cheered the crowd, even some of the Tuckertons themselves. The side had been retired without a run, and they cheered Cap's fine catch.

"Now for our last chance!" said Captain Graydon when his men came in. "We've just *got* to get two runs. No tenth inning—do it in this!"

"Sure!" they all agreed.

Whistle-Breeches came up first, and when he had fanned out he went off by himself and thought bitter thoughts. For he had narrowed the team's chances.

"Don't worry, we may do it yet," said the coach kindly but he hardly believed it.

Graydon made good in a two bagger, and got to third when Paul Armitage made a magnificent try, but was out at first. And that was the situation when Cap Smith came up. There were two out, a man on third, and two runs were needed. Only a home run it seemed could do the trick.

"And a home run it shall be!" declared Cap to himself.

But when he missed the first ball, and when, after two wild throws a strike was called on him, it looked as if the chances were all gone.

"He'll walk you!" shouted some sympathizers, but the Tuckerton pitcher had no such intentions. He was going to strike Cap out, he felt.

"Whizz!" went the ball toward the catcher. Cap drew back his bat, and by some streak of luck managed to get it under squarely. He put all the force of his broad shoulders into the blow, and when he saw the ball sailing far and low, he knew it would go over the centre fielder's head and into the deep grass beyond.

"It's a home run or a broken leg!" murmured Cap, as he dashed away toward first.

"Oh you Cap!"

"Pretty! Pretty!"

"A lalapalooza!"

"Run! Run!"

"Keep on going!"

"Come on in, Graydon! Come home! Come home!"

Thus the frantic cries.

Graydon was speeding in from third, and desperate fielders were racing after the ball. It could not be located in the tall grass, and Cap was legging it for all he was worth.

"Run! Run! Run!" Thus they besought him. Graydon crossed the rubber with the tying run, and still the ball was not found. Then, as Cap passed second, a shout announced that a fielder had it. But he was far out, and the second baseman knew his teammate could never field it in from where he was. He ran out to intercept the ball, as Cap was legging it for home.

"Thud!" The second baseman had the horsehide. He turned to throw it home, and the catcher spread out his hands for it. But Cap dropped and slid over the plate in a cloud of dust, and was safe just a second before the ball arrived.

Westfield had won! And on the last chance!

CHAPTER XVIII

A PLOT AGAINST BILL

WHAT rejoicing there was among the members of the nine and the supporters of the team! How the lads howled, their hoarse voices mingling with the shrill cries of the girls! Sober men danced around with their gray-haired seat-mates, and several "old grads" who had witnessed the contest jumped up and down pounding with their canes on the grandstand until it seemed as if the structure would collapse.

"Good boy, Cap!" cried Bill, clapping his brother on the back. "Good boy!"

"All to the horse radish," added Pete.

"Oh, you fellows didn't do so worse yourselves," remarked John, as he tried to fight off a crowd that wanted to carry him on their shoulders.

He was unsuccessful, and a moment later was hoisted up, while a shouting, yelling, cheering procession marched around the grounds, singing some of the old school songs of triumph. It was a glorious victory.

It was fought all over again in the rooms of the boys that night, and the team was praised on all sides.

"Still it was a narrow squeak," declared the coach to the captain, "and we've got to do better if we want to keep the championship."

"Oh, I guess we'll do it," answered Graydon. "Those Smith boys are a big find."

"I should say so! I don't know what to do about the battery, though. We can't let Mersfeld and Denby slide altogether."

"No, we'll have to play them occasionally. And Mersfeld isn't so bad sometimes. He gets rattled too easily, and Bill Smith doesn't. Well, come on out and I'll blow you to some chocolate soda."

Meanwhile the Smith boys were having a jollification of their own in their rooms, whither many of their friends had gone. Bill brought out some packages of cakes, and bottles of ginger ale and other soft stuff, on which the visitors were regaled.

"Here's more power to you!" toasted Billie Bunce, a little fat junior, who was not above making friends with the freshmen.

Mersfeld did not attend the little gathering in the rooms of our heroes. And had they seen him, in close conversation with Jonas North, a little later, and had they heard, what the two were saying, they would not have wondered at his absence. Mersfeld met North as the latter was strolling about the campus.

"What's going on up there?" asked North, as he motioned to where lights gleamed in the rooms of our friends, for it was not yet locking-up time.

"Oh, Smith Brothers and Company are having some sort of an improvised blow-out," replied the temporarily deposed pitcher. "Those fellows make me tired. Just because they helped pull one game out of the fire they think they're the whole cheese. I'd like to get square with Four-eyes somehow or other."

"Why don't you?" proposed North, with a grin. "Seems to me you ought to be able to 'do' him."

"I am, if it came to a fight, but I wouldn't dare mix it up with him."

"Why not?"

"Because there'd be a howl, and everyone would say I did it because I was jealous. I'd have to have some mighty good excuse to warrant wading into him."

"Well, can't you think of one?"

"No, I can't. I'd like to get square with him, though."

"Put him out of business you mean—so he couldn't pitch for a while?" asked the bully.

"That would do, yes."

"You might put up a job to burn his hands with acid in chemistry class some day. Just a little burn would do. You could say it was an accident."

"No, that's too risky," remarked Mersfeld, after thinking it over. "I'd like to have it come about naturally. Now if he or his brothers would try some trick, and get caught—suspended by the faculty for a month—or laid off from athletics, that would do. But the Smith fellows seem to have given up pranks lately, and have buckled down to lessons. I guess they're afraid."

North did not answer for a few moments. He walked along, apparently deeply thinking. Suddenly he exclaimed:

"I believe I have it! Get them caught while doing some fool cut-up thing, such as is always going on around here. That would do it, if we can get them into something desperate enough so they'll be suspended. Fine!"

"Yes, it's all very well enough to say 'fine!' But how are you going to work it? Haven't I told you that they've cut out jokes?"

"That's all right. We can get 'em into the game again."

"How?"

"Easy enough. All they need is to have some one to make a suggestion. They'll fall into line quickly enough, and then—have McNibb catch 'em in the act, and it's all off with their baseball. I haven't any love for 'em, either, and I'd like to see 'em out of the game. They don't belong in our class here."

"Oh, they're all right, but they think they're the whole show," complained the pitcher bitterly. "All I ask is for Bill Smith to get out of the box, and let me in. I can do as good as he!"

"Of course you can," agreed North, though if Mersfeld could have seen the covert sneer in the bully's smile perhaps he would not have been so friendly with him. "Well, if you'll help, I'll work it. We'll have 'em caught in the act—say painting the Weston statue red or green—that ought to fetch 'em."

"Yes, but how are you going to arrange to have 'em caught?" asked Mersfeld.

"Easy enough. Here's my game," went on North. "First we'll propose to Bill or Cap, or to the other brother, that as things around the school are a little dull, they ought to be livened up. They'll bite at the bait, for they like fun, and when they hear that it would be a good stunt to decorate the big bronze statue of old man Weston, in front of the main building with green or red paint, they'll fall for it."

"Yes, but they know enough not to get caught, even if they go into the trick."

"They can't help being caught the way we'll work it," was the crafty reply.

"Why not?"

"Because the night they select for the joke—and we'll know when it is—there'll be an anonymous letter dropped at Proctor McNibb's door, telling him what is going to be pulled off. He'll get on the job, and catch the Smith boys at the game. How's that?"

Mersfeld meditated a moment.

"I guess it will do," he said slowly—"only,—"

"Well, what's the matter with my plan?" demanded the bully half angrily.

"If you or I propose such a game to Bill or his brothers they'll smell a rat right away."

"Of course they will, but you don't s'pose I'm such a ninnie as to propose it ourselves; do you?"

"What then?"

"Why I'll have some one who is friendly to them do it. Oh, don't worry, they'll fall for it all right enough. Now come on over to my room, and we'll fix it up," and the two cronies, one a rather unwilling participator in the plot, walked along the campus, casting back a look at the gaily lighted windows of the apartments of the Smith boys.

"Hang it all!" mused Mersfeld as he tried to quiet an uneasy conscience, "I don't want to get those fellows into trouble, but I want to be back in my rightful place as pitcher on the Varsity."

And then he and North went into the details of the plot against our heroes, against Bill more particularly, for it was he whom Mersfeld wanted to displace.

CHAPTER XIX

THE PROFESSOR'S WARNING

"SAY, Cap, don't you think things are rather slow, not to say dreary around here?" asked Bob Chapin a few days after the ball game, as he strolled into the elder Smith lad's room, and appropriated the easiest chair. "It's the spring fever or the summer sleeping sickness coming on, I'm sure."

"What's up now, Bob?" asked Bill, as he tossed aside his chemistry, glad of an excuse to stop studying.

"What Bob needs is to train for the eleven or get into a baseball uniform," added Pete. "He's getting fat and lazy, and he hasn't any interest in life."

"Get out!" cried the visitor, who did not go in for athletics, and who preferred to be considered a "Sport," with a capital "S," wearing good clothes and spending all his spare time in a town billiard parlor. "You get out, Pete. Didn't I try for the glee club?"

"Yes, but you were too lazy to practice," remarked Cap frankly.

"How brutal of you!" cried Chapin, with a mock theatrical air. "Didn't I even forgive my enemies and beg them to take me into the banjo club?"

"Which, for the good of the service, they refused to do," went on the elder Smith.

"Oh, have you no mercy?" asked the visitor in a high falsetto voice, striking an attitude.

"We're all out of it—expect a fresh lot in next week," answered Bill. Then after a pause he added: "Now there's a thing you could do, Bob."

"What's that?"

Those Smith Boys on the Diamond

"Go in for theatricals. Why don't you join the Paint and Powder club?"

"Oh, I don't know. Afraid of spoiling my complexion with burnt cork and grease preparations, I guess," was the indolent reply. "But I don't want to discuss myself. I was asking if you fellows didn't find it dull here? Why, there hasn't been a thing pulled off since we brought the calf into the ancient history class two weeks ago. It is frightfully dull at Westfield. Don't you think so, really?"

"Hadn't noticed it," replied Cap. "What with baseball practice, and digging and boning and lectures and writing home occasionally for money we manage to exist; eh fellows?"

"Sure!" chorused his brothers.

"Well, I say it's dull," went on Chapin. "Now you fellows used to cut up some, when you first came, but you'd think you had all reformed the way you've been keeping quiet lately."

"There's nothing to do," complained Bill, in whom the spirit of mischief burned more strongly than in his brothers. "Show us a good lively time and we'll be in on it."

"I can't show it to you," replied Chapin. "You've got to make it for yourselves."

"Well, I'll do my share," went on Bill eagerly. "Why, is there something up?"

"Now, Bill, you haven't any time to undertake any pranks you know," admonished Cap, but his voice was not at all commanding, and there was a gleam of interest in his eyes.

"Yes, cut out the funny business," added Bill. "But what is it, anyhow, Bob? No harm in telling; is there?"

"Sure not. I was just wishing a racket would break loose, and I happened to think of something a while ago. It would take some nerve to do it though, and maybe you fellows—"

He paused significantly—temptingly.

"Say, who says we haven't got the nerve?" demanded Bill quickly.

"Now, Bill go easy," advised his older brother, but he, too, looked interested.

"Oh, well, certainly you have the nerve," admitted Chapin. "But it's risky."

"Are you willing to go in on it?" asked Pete quickly.

"Of course," was the instant rejoinder.

"Then name your game!" came from Bill, "and you'll find us right behind you up to the muzzle of the cannon. Out with it!"

"Oh, I wish you'd stayed away," spoke Cap. "I'm back in my trigonometry, and if I flunk—Well, I suppose we may as well hear what you've got up your sleeve," and he laid aside his book, with a laugh and a half-protesting shake of his head.

Bob's first act was to go over to the door of Cap's room, in which the gathering took place, and see that the portal was tightly closed. Then he listened at the keyhole.

"Is it perfectly safe?" he asked in a whisper. "Can anyone hear us?"

"Say, what are we up against?" asked Cap with a laugh. "Is this a gunpowder plot, or merely a scheme to burn the old school."

"Listen, and I will a tale unfold," went on Chapin. "Gather 'round, my children, gather 'round the camp-fire and Anthony shall tell us one of his famous stories. So they gathered 'round—"

"Oh, get along with it—we've got to do some boning to-night, Bob," complained Pete. "We've heard that camp-fire joke before."

"Do you know the bronze statue of 'Pop' Weston in front of the school?" asked the visitor in a stage whisper.

"Do we know it? The statue of the founder of Westfield? Well I should bust a bat but we do," answered Bill.

"What do you think of the color of it?" asked Chapin.

"What do you mean?" Cap wanted to know.

"I mean wouldn't it look prettier red or blue or pink, than the shade it is now?"

He paused to look at the three brothers. They did not answer for a moment. Then Bill exclaimed:

"Say, is that what you mean—to paint the statue?"

Chapin nodded slowly.

"It's—sacrilege," whispered Cap.

"Only an iconoclast would dare think of such a thing," declared Bill. "But—" there was an eager light in his eyes.

"It was done once, years ago," proceeded the tempter, "and the whole Freshman class was suspended for a week, as the faculty couldn't find out who did it. It has been many, many, weary years since such an honor fell upon us Freshmen," and he sighed deeply, as though in pain.

"By Jove!" exclaimed Cap softly. The daring plot appealed to him, conservative as he was.

"How did they get the paint off?" asked Pete.

"It had to wear off," replied Chapin. "But I don't want to do anything like that. We can use water colors, and they won't spoil the bronze, and really it would be a little too rotten to make such a mess of it. Just tint it a light Alice blue, or a dainty Helen pink—it will wash off, but it will look pretty for a while, and the freshmen class will have made a name for itself that it can be proud of. Are you with me? It can easily be done, and the chances are we won't be caught. How about it?"

"I'll do it!" exclaimed Bill quickly.

"I don't know," began Cap.

"Oh, come on," urged Pete. "It's been a long time since we've had any fun."

"If we're caught, it means good-bye to balls and bats," went on the eldest brother.

"But we won't be caught," declared Chapin eagerly. "Besides, what if we are—that's half the fun."

"All right, go ahead," agreed Cap. "Might as well be killed for a sheep as a lamb, I guess. I'm in on it."

"Now about the paint," went on the tempter, as he again listened at the door. "We'll have to be careful where we get it, as McNibb is a regular detective for following a clue. It ought to be bought out of town."

"That's so," agreed Pete.

"Hold on, I have it!" cried Bill, after a moment's thought. "Professor Clatter."

"Professor Clatter?" inquired Chapin. "You mean that medicine man with his queer wagon?"

"Exactly," went on the pitcher. "I saw him in town the other day, and he said he was coming back to play a return engagement near here. He's got some new kind of stomach dope or something like that. Besides, he has some patent face powder that he says he got at a bargain, and he's going to try and work it off on the ladies in the crowd. It's a beautiful pink, and it's harmless. I was looking at a box of it, and it got on my hands. Say, for a few minutes I had the nicest baby complexion you'd want to see. But it all washed off as easily as soap."

"Well, what's the answer?" asked Chapin, as Bill paused.

"Why we'll get some of that powder from the professor, mix it up, and use it on the statute. It will come off easily and I defy Proctor McNibb to trace where it came from. The professor is a friend of ours, and he'll keep mum."

"The very thing!" cried the visitor. "When can you get it?"

"To-morrow, or next day," answered Bill, who had now entered heart and soul into the piece of mischief. "I'll get enough to give Pop Weston a liberal coating."

"Night after to-morrow," mused Chapin, looking at a calendar over Cap's table. "That will do. There's no moon. What about brushes?"

"I guess a whitewash one will do. Maybe the professor has one—or a big sponge, such as he uses for cleaning his wagon."

"Fine!" cried Chapin. "Oh, I can just see the faculty when they file past the bronze statue, done to a beautiful baby pink! Great! No more will the lordly Seniors boast of having once run a dump cart into the class room. The Sophs with their little trick of putting tar on the bell tower will take a back seat, and the Juniors, whose stronghold, so far, has been the horrible task of burning red fire under Prexy's windows, will be green with envy. Oh, what a lucky day this has been!"

"It isn't over yet," remarked Cap significantly.

"Well, I'll see Clatter and get the stuff," promised Bill. "Then we'll meet and do the decorating. How many are in on it?" asked the pitcher, pausing in his planning.

"We don't want too many," spoke Chapin cautiously. "Us four perhaps, Bondy and Whistle-Breeches if you like, as they're on this corridor."

"Not Bondy," said Pete quickly. "We'll let Whistle-Breeches in, but Guilder isn't in our set. He wouldn't come if we asked him, and we're not going to. Besides, he might squeal."

"Well, five are enough," said Chapin. "Now I'll depend on you to get the paint, Bill."

"And I'll get it."

"Fare thee well, then," and with another cautious listening at the door, Chapin took himself out.

"Well?" asked Cap, of his brothers a little later, when they had sat in silence pondering over the plan.

"It's all to the red-pepper," declared Bill. "We need something to wake us up."

"I guess this will prevent dreams for some time," observed the eldest Smith.

"It'll be a scream of a nightmare when the faculty sees it," came from Pete, "but there's no harm in it as long as the paint washes off."

With many nods and winks Chapin recalled to the three brothers, and to Whistle-Breeches, next morning the plot they had made. Whistle-Breeches had been let into it early in the day, and had eagerly agreed to do his share. They would need ropes with which to mount to the top of the big statue, and Anderson had agreed to procure them.

"I can climb, too," he said, "and I'll decorate the top part."

"Good for you, Whistle-Breeches!" exclaimed Pete.

It was that same afternoon that Bill saw Bob Chapin in close conversation with Mersfeld and Jonas North. It was the first time he had noticed that Chapin was chummy with the Varsity regular pitcher, and with the lad who, because of his bullying tactics was generally shunned, except by his own crowd.

"I hope Bob doesn't talk too much about the statue business," reflected Bill. "Too many cooks make the hash taste burned. It might leak out."

Then, as he was summoned to practice he gave the matter no more thought until that evening, when he set off alone to see Professor Clatter, and get the pink paint.

Pete and Cap wanted to accompany him, but Bill declared that there was safety in small numbers, and that he preferred to go alone.

He found his old friend getting ready for an evening performance, filling his gasoline torches, looking over his stock of supplies, and tuning the banjo with which, and his not unmelodious voice, he drew a throng about the gaily painted wagon.

"Ha, my young friend, back again!" cried the professor. "Greetings to you. And where are the brothers?"

"Studying, I expect, or making a pretense to."

"Good again! Ah, the lamp of learning burns brightly when one is young. What ho! Mercurio! Some more gasoline for this torch! We must have light!" Then the professor having ordered about an imaginary slave, proceeded to fill the torch himself.

"Speaking of lamps of learning," broke in Bill, thinking this was a good time to announce his errand, "we're going to do a little illumination over at Westfield on our own account. How much of that pink paint have you, Professor?"

"Pink paint—you mean my Matchless Complexion Tinting Residuum?"

"I guess that's it. We need some."

"For a masked ball?"

"For a bronze statue," replied Bill, and he proceeded to relate the details of the plot. The professor listened carefully. Bill told everything, and at length the traveling vendor asked:

"Did you and your brothers think of this scheme, Bill?"

"No, as a matter of fact Bob Chapin proposed it."

"Ah, I suppose he is one of the leading spirits when it comes to these plots of—er—innocent mischief?"

"No, I never knew him to get up anything of the kind before. And that's the funny part of it. He never takes a hand in 'em. But now he comes to us with the idea, and he's going to help carry it out. I never knew he had gumption enough to break out this way. It's a good one, though."

"And doesn't it strike you as odd that he suddenly breaks out now?" asked the professor in rather a curious voice.

"Odd? Dow do you mean?"

"I mean do you think he had any object in it?"

"Object in it?"

"Yes, to get you boys interested and—"

"Why, he's interested himself. He's going to help decorate Pop Weston."

"I know, but you say he never did anything of the kind before," objected Mr. Clatter, looking sharply at Bill.

"No."

"And isn't it rather late in the college year for him to begin?"

"It is—say, look here, Professor Clatter! Do you know anything about this?" demanded Bill.

"No, only what my common sense tells me. But I gather that there is some feeling against you because of baseball matters."

"A little—yes, Mersfeld is sore, but—"

"Wait a minute. Now, if some of your enemies could get you into a game like this, and then desert you, and let the whole blame fall on you, or, even, we'll say, tip off the college authorities, to use a slang term—wouldn't they make trouble for you."

"Yes, they would, but—"

"Is this Bob Chapin a particular friend of yours?"

"Not particularly."

"Is he in with this Mersfeld?"

"No, not any more than—By Jove!" Bill checked himself suddenly. The remembrance of Chapin talking earnestly to Mersfeld and North came back to him.

"Ah!" exclaimed the professor knowingly, as he rubbed his hands. "I fancy we are getting at something. Now if our friend Tithonus Somnus were here we would get him to read the stars for us, but, in his absence I'll venture to give you a bit of advice, Bill."

"What is it, Mr. Clatter."

"You may consider this in the light of a warning," went on the medicine vendor earnestly. "Don't have anything to do with the trick of painting the statue, Bill; or if you do—"

He paused significantly.

"Well, if we do?" repeated Bill.

"If you do, then play the double cross, and catch your enemies in the net they have spread for you," was the reply in a low voice.

Bill started, and, as he did so there came a cautious knock at the door of the wagon.

"Who's there?" asked the professor quickly.

"It's me—Tithonus," was the answer in a hoarse whisper. "Let me in—quick! The police are after me!"

CHAPTER XX

THE PLOTTERS CAUGHT

Professor Clatter swung wide the door, and the figure of the rain-maker toppled in, rather than walked.

"Quick! Shut it and lock it!" he cried, and he assisted in the operation. Then he passed beyond the small room in the rear of the wagon—a room that served as dining hall, living apartment, sitting room and parlor, and in a few seconds Mr. Somnus could be heard crawling into one of the bunks.

"If they come for me—you haven't seen me, of course," came his voice in muffled tones, indicating that his head was under the bed clothes.

"Of course not, my dear Tithy," replied the professor. "And, in fact, so quick was your passage through, like a half back making a touchdown, to use a phrase doubtless familiar to my friend Bill Smith—to use that phrase, I have scarcely seen you. But what is the matter? Why this haste? There doesn't seem to be any one following you—at least not at your heels."

"Are you sure?" asked the muffled voice.

"Sure, yes, Tithy," replied the medicine man, after a moment of listening. "No one is coming. But what in the world is the matter?"

"Oh, it's an unfortunate mistake I made," was the answer. "If you'll wait a while, to make sure the police and sheriffs officers are not after me, I'll come out and explain."

"I wish you would, Tithy, for Bill and I are much in the dark."

After a wait of several minutes, during which Bill wondered what in the world could have caused the rain-maker to flee in such terror, the individual in question came out of the compartment devoted to the sleeping bunks.

"Well?" asked the professor.

"Not well—bad," was the despondent reply. "You see I found the star-gazing trade poor lately, on account of so many cloudy nights, so, in order to make a living I ventured to proclaim that I would read the stars and reveal the future—for a consideration. It was risky, I know, but I did it, and did it well—for a time.

"All was prosperous and happy, until to-night, just before supper I was visited by a man who wanted to know whether he would be successful in a certain undertaking. I consulted my charts and said that he would."

"What was the undertaking?" asked Bill.

"He was going to collect a long overdue bill from a man who owed him some money," went on the astronomer. "I told him to be firm, and he would succeed.

"A little later he came back, all tattered and torn, with one eye blackened, his collar a rag, and his clothes covered with dirt. He entered my wagon without knocking, and presented himself before me.

"'I was firm!' he shouted at me, 'but I did not succeed. This is what the other man did to me!' Oh, it was terrible. He accused me of deceiving him, and he sprang at me, and would doubtless have made me suffer, but I escaped through the front door, leaving my beloved cat, Scratch, behind, and I fled here.

"As I ran on I could hear the terrible threats the man uttered against me, of causing my arrest. Even now I fear—hark! What's that?"

Mr. Somnus paused in alarm, and seemed about to dart for the bunks again.

"Nothing—absolutely nothing," answered the professor, calmly. Mr. Somnus listened, and seemed satisfied.

"I guess that fellow didn't mean all he said," put in Bill.

"Perhaps," agreed the astronomer, with a sigh. "I certainly hope not."

"You are not the only one who has troubles," went on the traveling medicine man. "Here's Bill."

"What troubles has he?" asked Mr. Somnus. "Has he been predicting—reading the stars?"

"Not exactly," answered the pitcher. And then Professor Clatter told about the proposed painting of the statue and his own warning.

"I'm glad you happened in, Tithy," went on the vendor of the Peerless Permanent Pain Preventative, "for I'd like your opinion about this matter. I say it's a plot to get Bill and his brothers into trouble, what do you think about it?" He detailed the reasons for his suspicions, and waited for an answer.

"Well," began the fugitive, "not speaking by the stars at all, you understand, and making no promises for which I can be held responsible, I think you're right, Theophilus. And I'd advise Bill to look out."

"But how?" eagerly asked the pitcher. "I'm beginning to agree with you. How can I catch Mersfeld and North at their little game, for a game I think it is?"

"Easy enough," said the professor. "Go on as if you and your brothers and Whistle-Breeches—Oh, what a classical name—go on as if you intended to carry out the trick. Take my word for it those fellows will be hidden somewhere ready to see you caught, and you can turn the tables on them.

"In some way they will, I feel sure, get word to the college authorities of what is on foot. Very well, you have but to stay away at the last moment, and give some sign by which the proctor will be led to the hiding place of your enemies. Then, by judiciously spilling a little of the pink paint near their rooms, and secreting a pot of it near their hiding place, you will have them on the hip, as my friends the Romans say."

"Good!" cried Bill, after a moment's thought, "I'll do it."

"Then here is the pink powder," went on the professor, handing Bill several packages, "and may luck attend you. Just mix it with water, and it will do the work. Now, Tithy, I can attend to your case."

"And I'll get back to school, and put up a game on North and Mersfeld," said Bill.

"We wish we could be there to see," spoke Mr. Clatter in eager tones. "Tithy and I would enjoy it, but we have troubles of our own. I'll be around this way in about two weeks again, and you can tell me about it."

"Come to the ball game," invited Bill. "We're going to play Sandrim in a league contest."

"I will, if I am not in jail," promised the astronomer solemnly.

Bill hurried back to his brothers and told his story, adding the professor's suspicions, warnings and advice.

"The sneaks!" burst out Cap. "Mersfeld and North to put up a game like that on us."

"And Chapin to go in with them," added Pete.

"They ought to be run out of school!" declared Whistle-Breeches.

"Easy," suggested Bill. "Maybe Bob Chapin didn't know what he was up against. We'll have a talk with him."

Bob soon proved to the satisfaction of the Smith brothers and Donald Anderson, that he was not aware of the "double cross" plan of the deposed Varsity pitcher.

"North and Mersfeld suggested the scheme to me," Bob admitted, "and said you fellows would be good ones to do it."

"And they're going to play a safety, and hide somewhere to watch us be nabbed by McNibb; aren't they?" demanded Cap.

"They're going to hide some place near the statue," replied Bob, "because I heard them saying something about it. But, honest, fellows, I didn't know that they were going to squeal. They got me all worked up and I was interested. I hope you believe me."

"We do," Bill assured him. "Now to get even. I guess, in case they make the split, that they'll send an anonymous letter to McNibb. How about it?"

"Naturally," agreed Cap and Pete.

"Then we'll add another," went on Bill, "and in it we'll disclose the hiding place of the sneaks. Where did you say it would be, Bob?"

"In the clump of rhododendron bushes in front of the statue."

"Good! Now the plot thickens, and we'll have to thicken the pink paint. Come on, fellows, get busy. First I'll prepare the second anonymous letter."

A few hours later Proctor McNibb was rather surprised to receive a screed, signed with no name, informing him that a plot existed among a certain lot of Freshmen, and that the said plot consisted of a plan to paint the founder's statue baby-pink.

"If you wish to catch the vandals, be on hand near the statue shortly after midnight," the anonymous epistle went on.

Now the proctor was an honorable man, and usually did not pay much attention to unsigned letters. But here was one he felt that he must heed. Where it had come from he did not bother his head about.

"Some upper classmen, who have given over such sacrilegious horse-play may have sent it," he argued, "or the townsman from whom the paint was purchased may have been stricken with remorse, or have a fear that he will be found out. At any rate I'll catch them red-handed. No, pink-handed I guess," and the proctor smiled at his joke.

The official's surprise may be imagined when, shortly after the receipt of the first letter, he got another. Our friends had a spy, in the person of one of the janitors, who did work in that part of the school where Mr. McNibb had his rooms, and the janitor at once informed Bill when there were signs of unusual activity in the proctor's office.

"It's their letter!" declared Bill. "Now for ours!" and it was sent, disclosing the information that the would-be painters of the statue would be hidden in the clump of rhododendron bushes.

Then there was a busy time for our friends. Throwing in his lot with the Smith boys and Whistle-Breeches, Bob Chapin helped them in the plot, by pretending to keep Mersfeld and North posted.

"You can hide in the bushes, just as you planned," said the languid youth to them.

"And see the fun?" eagerly asked Mersfeld. "Will they be on hand?"

"Oh, they'll be on hand all right," said Bob, and there was a grim smile on his face, which the plotters did not observe.

So anxious were they to be present, and see the Smith boys captured, that Mersfeld and North left their rooms early. This was the cue for Bill and his brothers to make their way to the enemies' apartments, and, by scattering around a little of the pink mixture, give the idea, to a casual observer, that the coloring stuff had been prepared there.

In the meanwhile, and before the two lads who had planned to get their classmates in trouble had gone to their hiding place, several pails of the pink mixture had been hidden in the clump of bushes. Strings led from the pails to behind a stone wall, where Bill, his brothers, together with Whistle-Breeches and Bob, would hide. At the proper time the strings would be pulled, and the stuff upset. This would be additional evidence against the two plotters.

"Well, I guess it's about time for us to go out," said Cap, as midnight approached, that hour, having been suggested to Bob by the plotters. "Go easy, now, for McNibb may have spotters posted."

"No, I think not," said Bob. "He'll depend on catching us at the statue. Oh, wow! Won't those fellows be surprised!"

Mersfeld and North were in hiding. They had been waiting for some time.

"Hang it all!" muttered the deposed Varsity pitcher, "why don't they come?"

"Oh, they'll be here all right."

"You don't s'pose they could have backed out; do you?"

"No, Bob Chapin said they were hot for the trick, and rose to it like a hungry trout to a fly. Oh, they'll be here."

"Then I wish they'd hurry. I'm getting a cramp in my leg, crouching down so long."

"That's nothing. I know I'll have rheumatism or housemaid's knee, or something like it, for sitting on the damp ground. But think of it! They'll be suspended, and you'll be back on the nine!"

"Yes, that makes it worth while."

"Hark! I think I hear something!" cried North suddenly.

They peered out. Two dark figures could be seen coming cautiously around the base of the statue.

"That's them!" whispered Mersfeld.

"No, that's McNibb, and one of the janitors is with him. He's too early! He'll scare 'em off!"

"Jove! It looks so. I wonder—"

"Say! He's heading this way!" cried North suddenly. "Can he see us?"

They waited in an agony of fear and apprehension. There was a movement in the bushes—a curious sloshing, splashing sound, and something seemed to be flowing around the feet of the two plotters.

"Great guns!" cried Mersfeld, "what are we up against?"

"Keep quiet," begged North hoarsely.

It was too late.

"Ha! I have you! Waiting for a chance to despoil the statue; are you?" cried the voice of the proctor.

He made a rush for the bushes. Mersfeld and North made a rush to get out. Their feet became entangled in the strings that had been pulled a moment before by the hidden Smith boys. Down in the pink paint went the conspirators, just as the proctor and his impressed aide hurried up and grabbed them.

"I have you!" exclaimed the college official. "I have stopped your nefarious work just in time. Strike a match, Biddel."

The janitor obeyed. In the glow stood two sorry-looking figures, pink paint dripping from them.

"Mersfeld and North!" ejaculated the proctor. "I would not have believed a member of the Varsity nine capable of such a trick."

"We weren't going to do it," began the pitcher, and then the futility of the denial made itself plain to him, as in the dying glow of the match he saw the sight he and his companion presented.

"Follow me, gentlemen," said the proctor simply, leading the way to his quarters.

"Caught in their own trap!" whispered Bill softly, as he and his brothers and chums looked over the top of the wall, and saw what had taken place.

"Talk about painting the town red," murmured Cap. "The very *grass* is *pink*, over there," and chuckling to themselves our heroes hurried to their rooms lest they, too, be taken in for being out after hours.

CHAPTER XXI

AN INTERRUPTED SUPPER

"Wasn't it great?" demanded Bill.

"All to the lalapalooza!" was Cap's opinion.

"I thought sure McNibb would hear us snickering when we pulled the strings and upset the paint," added Pete.

"And what a sight Mersfeld and North were!" remarked Whistle-Breeches. "They must have looked like walking complexion advertisements when the lights were turned on."

"I wonder if they'll be fired?" spoke Bob Chapin. "I wouldn't like that."

"Hu! That's probably what they wanted to happen to us!" cut in Whistle-Breeches. "It's a case of chicken eat turkey I reckon, and everybody have cranberries."

"They didn't actually *do* anything," went on Bill, as he and his brothers and chums were talking over the affair next morning. "The evidence only pointed to them as if they were *going* to do it."

"That's enough for McNibb," commented Cap. "Great monkey doodles! There goes last bell and I've got to look over my Pindar yet. Holy mackerel!"

The whole school was buzzing with the news, and it was soon generally known that the Smith boys had neatly turned the tables on the plotters.

As for those worthies, the events had followed each other so rapidly that they hardly knew what to think, much less say or do. It was a complete surprise to them, and they dared not utter a word as to what their real intentions had been.

As Cap had said, the circumstantial evidence was enough against them. They had been caught, if not exactly with the paint in their possession, at least with it all over them, and the anonymous letter was enough to declare their object, albeit that screed was intended to throw suspicions on others.

"Have you anything to say?" the proctor had asked them when he had them in his sanctum.

"I—er—I guess not," answered North, with a glance at his pink-stained clothing.

"How about you, Mersfeld?"

"I—I don't know, it was not our intention—Oh, well, I guess I have nothing to say, either," and the pitcher gave up the attempt.

"Very well. You may go. I'll take your case up with the faculty."

The two lads were in an agony of apprehension lest they be expelled, or suspended for the remainder of the term, but after a faculty meeting, in which Dr. Burton had made a plea for them, it was decided to debar both lads from participation in all athletic or other sports for a month, to stop all evening leave for the same period, and to inflict other punishment in the matter of doing extra classical study.

The fact that they had not actually committed any overt act of sacrilege against the statue was in their favor, though, as the proctor said, only the receipt of the anonymous letter prevented it.

And how Mersfeld and his crony writhed in agony as they thought of the letter they had themselves written! They guessed that their plot had been laid bare, and they suspected Bob Chapin, who, fearing punishment, spoke to the Smith boys about it. Then, on Cap's suggestion, and in order that the truth might be known, a statement of how it had all come about was drawn up and sent to the two plotters.

"That's the last time I try any of *your* tricks," said Mersfeld bitterly to North.

"Get out! Weren't you as hot for it as I was? Why don't you think of something yourself then, if you're so smart?"

"I will—next time," and the two parted not the best of friends.

The barring of Mersfeld from the diamond took him off the Varsity team for the time being, though he was still considered a member of it, even if he could not play. He was allowed to take part in practice games, however, for Captain Graydon and Coach Windam well knew the value of keeping some box men in reserve.

"No telling when Smith will develop a glass arm or go up in the air, or get wild," said Graydon.

"No, but he's doing well now," declared the coach. "He pitched a no-hit-no-run game in a five inning practice the other day."

"That's too good to last. We've got to hold on to Mersfeld, and work up some one else."

"Sure. Mighty queer how the Smith boys turned that statue trick; eh?"

"Oh, those fellows aren't greenhorns, if they did come from the country. Wait until they get hold of the ropes here a little better, and they'll cut things loose."

"Yes, and maybe they'll be barred from the team."

But our heroes showed no inclinations, at present, of doing anything like that. They went on the even tenor of their ways, showed up regularly at baseball practice, and had their lessons as well, perhaps, as the average student. They did not "cut" more than the regulation number of lectures, and they made many friends.

Bill kept on improving in his control and his curve work, until the delighted coach and captain declared that they already had a good grip on the pennant.

Several unimportant games were played, and one or two of the league contests, in which the Westfield nine made about an even break. The season was far from over, and he would indeed have been a wise prophet who could have told who would win the pennant.

"I think even Duodecimo Donaldby, alias Tithonus Somnus himself would be at a loss," declared Cap. "But, fellows," he went on, addressing his two brothers, "keep up the good work. Make the name of 'Smith' a credit to the school."

"The only trouble is that there are so many Smiths that in ages to come they won't know which breed it was who did it," complained Pete.

Mersfeld was bitter in his heart against our heroes, and was anxious for revenge, but he and North had had a falling out, and he did not know what he could do to get even with the Smith boys. Meanwhile he sulked in his room, and thought mean thoughts.

"Say, fellows, do you know I think we ought to do something," remarked Bill to his brothers one day, as they came in tired but happy from the diamond, after some hard practice. "It's been dull lately."

"Yes, let's paint another statue," remarked Cap grimly.

"Or put a cow in the physics class," suggested Pete.

"No, but seriously, I think it's up to us to do something," went on Bill. "We've got a lot of friends who expect things from us, and we ought to keep up our reputation. What do you say that we give a little spread? Dad sent me two fivers the other day."

"You can't give a spread for that," declared Cap.

"I know it, but you fellows have some, and if you loosen up a bit—"

"Oh, count us in," came quickly from Pete, "only how are you going to do it? Hire a hall in town, and—"

"Oh, not that kind!" cried Bill quickly. "I mean a little midnight supper up in our rooms. We can do it fine here, as we're on the same floor. It's like one big room when the connecting doors are open."

"We'd get caught sure as blazes," observed Cap, "and you know our reputations are none too good. I think McNibb suspects us of having something to do with the statue game."

"Why?" asked Bill.

"Oh, the other day he was up here, snooping around, and he saw a splash of that pink paint on the wall. He went over to it right away, and looked at it like Sherlock Holmes. I was in a nervous sweat, and I thought he'd ask some questions, but he only said: 'Ah, Smith, that color has a powerful spreading ability; hasn't it?'"

"And what did you say?" demanded Bill.

"What *could* I say? Nothing. I just played safety and kept still, and mighty glad I was that he didn't ask any more. But as I say, I think he suspects us, so we've got to be careful."

"Oh, we can pull this off all right," declared Bill. "I have a plan."

"Tell it," begged Whistle-Breeches. "Things are dull of late. Liven 'em up."

He had entered just in time to hear Bill's last remark.

"Well, some big-gun from the other side, England or Germany, is coming here next Friday night, to lecture on pedagogics or something like that. The entire faculty is going, I understand, and only McNibb and the janitors will be on hand. Besides that, the Seniors have some sort of a legitimate blow out, and there's the Junior concert. So things will be quiet around here, and we can just as well as not have our spread. What do you say, fellows?"

"I'm for it—here's my cash," answered Pete, passing over some bills.

"Ditto," added Cap, following suit.

"Say, fellows, I'm broke," put in Bob Chapin, who looked in at that juncture, "but if there's anything like that going on, count me in."

"Me too!" cried Whistle-Breeches.

"This is strictly on the Smith boys," declared Bill. "It's to celebrate our second childhood, or something like that. Well, I'll go ahead with the arrangements."

Those Smith Boys on the Diamond

On the Friday night in question there might have been seen a number of figures—dark, stealthy figures—stealing, one at a time, toward the dormitory where the Smith boys lived and moved and had their being. Yet not a gleam of light shone from their windows, for Bill had bought some black roofing paper and tacked it over the casements.

"It makes it warm," he said, "but it's safer."

The good things had been bought, and some boards to be covered with newspapers and laid on the beds were to serve for tables. As the lights were turned off at a certain hour, save in the corridor, candles had been procured.

"At last all was in readiness," as they say in novels. The guests had assembled and were gathered about the banquet table. No one had been caught, as yet, for Bill had laid his plans well, and all of the faculty, some of whom might otherwise have been prowling about the school, were listening to a very deep lecture on how to impart knowledge to boys, by a man who had never had any. As for Proctor McNibb, he had so many extra duties on his hands that he did not go near the Freshmen's dormitory until quite late.

This gave our heroes and their friends the lack of attention which they much desired. There was a goodly crowd present, when Whistle-Breeches, who had been named as toastmaster, arose, and with a bottle of ginger ale in one hand, and a cheese sandwich in the other, proposed:

"Those Smith boys! May we always have 'em with us!"

"Hear! Hear!" cried Wendell Borden, in a dull, monotonous voice. Wendell had read that this was what Englishmen said at banquets, and his father had come from England.

"Less noise!" ordered Bill. "Do you want to have the place pulled, and all of us pinched? Go on and eat!"

They fell-to, and there was merry feasting, even if the jests did have to be passed around in whispers, losing thereby much of their wit.

"Now, fellows," began Bob Chapin, as he rose and held out a bottle of lemon soda, "let me propose—"

There was a knock on the door—a knock as of one having authority.

A sudden hush fell upon the assemblage.

"Answer, Bill, Cap—some of you," whispered Whistle-Breeches nervously.

"What'll I say?" demanded Bill.

The knock was repeated.

"Ask whose there," suggested Bob.

"Who—who's—there?" stammered Bill, as though it cost him an effort.

"It is I—Mr. McNibb. Are there any persons in your room besides yourselves?"

"Ye—yes," stammered Bill. Lying was not permitted by the school honor code.

"Open the door!" came the command.

Bill looked appealingly around. Some of the boys made motions as though to dive under the beds.

"Face the music!" ordered Cap sharply, for he detested sneaking tactics.

"Open the door," came the command again, in stern tones.

There was no choice but to obey, and Bill arose to draw the bolts.

He slowly opened the portal, and, as it swung back the banqueters peered forward to behold the smiling countenances of Ward and Merton, two of the biggest seniors in the school.

CHAPTER XXII

HITTING A BULLY

BLANK looks of surprise, astonishment, relief and anger at the manner in which they had been deceived, struggled for mastery over the faces of the Freshmen. The two seniors walked in, looked coolly about, as though the whole affair had been arranged for their especial entertainment and inspection, and then calmly took two vacant seats near the head of the improvised banquet table, which is to say the bed.

"Ah, very cozy and comfortable here; eh Ward?" observed Merton.

"Indeed yes. The old Romans weren't in it with these chaps. They don't recline at table, but make their table on the recline! Ha! Ha! Joke! Everybody laugh!"

There was a grim silence, at which the Seniors seemed surprised. They looked around at the banqueters.

"Well, why don't you laugh?" demanded Ward. "Don't you Freshies know what's good for you?"

"Ha! Ha!" burst out Bill, as much in relief at not finding McNibb in their midst, as at the alleged joke.

"Laugh!" commanded Merton sternly.

"Laugh!" ordered Ward sharply.

It was instruction that could not be disobeyed, for the Freshmen, under certain circumstances, were by the unwritten, but none the less stringent rules of the school, bound to do certain things commanded by their class superiors. Thereupon there ensued a series of snickers, more or less forced.

"Not so loud!" ordered Merton. "Or you *will* have McNibb here. Sorry if we gave you fellows heart-failure, but we smelled out this little feed, and thought we'd better show you how easy it is to get caught. Pass the cheese."

"And I'll have some of those pickled lambs tongues," added Ward. "I say, boys, you *do* know how to get up a grub-fest. Who's doing?"

"The Smith boys," murmured Whistle-Breeches.

"Might have known," declared Merton. "Say, you fellows are cutting things loose at Westfield. Well, it's good for the old school. Here, Ward, are some prime macaroons."

The seniors helped themselves and each other to what was best on the table, making more or less funny remarks, while their unwilling hosts looked on, not daring, because of another unwritten law, to eat with them.

"Here, get busy, you fellows," ordered Ward. "Pass things up toward this end. We're hungry, and it isn't often that you have two noble Roman senators to grace your banquets. Get busy."

"What appetites!" murmured Cap in whispered admiration. "I thought I could eat, but they have me beaten a mile."

"Never mind, as long as it wasn't McNibb. They're welcome to all that's left—we had a good share," spoke Bill.

The Seniors seemed to be having a good time, but they could not keep on eating, and even in their hearts was the fear lest they be caught. So, with a mock farewell, they took their departure, promising to send some of their fellows around to enjoy the feast of good things.

But no more of the fourth-year men arrived, due to the fact, probably, that the meeting at which were the entire faculty, was nearly at an end, and soon the college and the grounds would be infested by professors. Then, too McNibb might come around at any moment.

"Hurry, fellows," suggested Bill and his brothers. "Eat what's left and then cut out of here. It *might* be McNibb next time."

"Say, I thought it was all up with us, when that knock came," remarked Pete.

"Same here," added Whistle-Breeches. "Are there any stuffed olives left?"

"Nary a one," answered Cap. "Those chaps stuffed themselves on 'em."

"Stuffed Seniors instead of stuffed olives," observed Bill grimly.

The feast was over, the remains cleared away and, one by one, or in couples, the guests departed, with intervals between the leavings, so that too much noise might not be created.

The last one had gone—the room was in fairly good shape, albeit bottles and cans had been piled into closets until the recesses were almost overflowing—there to stay until such time as they could be smuggled out.

"Well; how about it?" asked Bill.

"It was all right—even the interruption," replied Cap.

There came a sudden knock on the door. The brothers, who were not the only occupants of their adjoining rooms looked at each other with fear in their eyes.

"Gentlemen, are you in bed?" demanded the unmistakable voice of the proctor.

"Ye—yes!" exclaimed Bill, making an appealing motion to his brothers. With a single motion they threw themselves, dressed as they were, upon the covers, while Bill extinguished the single candle. "We're in bed, Mr. McNibb."

"I'm glad to hear it," was the grim retort. "I thought I saw a light through the key hole."

"No—no, sir," declared Pete. The room was in darkness but the smell of a recently extinguished candle was only too evident.

Those Smith Boys on the Diamond

"Very well," and the proctor passed on, leaving the Smith boys to recover of near-heart-failure as best they might.

The banquet given by our heroes was the talk of the school for several days—wireless talk, of course, for it would never do to have it come to the ears of those in authority. Those who had not been favored with an invitation were wondering how they could cultivate the good graces of our friends, and the lucky ones who had attended were wondering when there would be another spread.

There was hard baseball practice the day following the little affair, and, for some reason Bill was a little off in his pitching.

"You'll either have to get a new pair of glasses," grimly remarked the coach, "or you'll have to cut out your midnight suppers, Smith."

"All right," agreed the pitcher, for the word of Mr. Windam was law. The scrub, on which Mersfeld was pitching was close to beating the Varsity, over which fact the deposed twirler was gloating.

"If things go on this way," he said to his crony North, as they left the field, the two again being friendly, "I'll be back in the box once more."

"I'd be glad to help you," was the answer, for though North did not exactly care for Mersfeld, whom he felt was not in his "class," yet the bully had formed an unreasoning hate toward our heroes, and would have been glad to see them run out of the school. "If anything turns up by which we can get back at those fellows, count me in."

"All right," replied Mersfeld, duly grateful.

The two strolled across the campus, and, as they got behind a clump of bushes, North saw a small, timid boy, one of the students at a preparatory school connected with Westfield, passing along. He called to the lad, whom he knew slightly:

"Here, Harvey, carry my glove and bat, I'm tired," for North had been playing on the scrub.

"Oh, please, I can't," replied Harvey. "I'm in a hurry. I—I will next time."

"I said now!" exclaimed North putting out a hand, and catching the small chap roughly by the shoulder. "*Now*, do you hear! Not next week, but *now*. What's getting into you fellows from the prep, anyhow? Take that bat!" and the bully brought it down with considerable force on Harvey's shoulder.

The little lad gave a cry of pain, and started to run, breaking from North's hold. With a coarse expression the larger student threw his heavy glove at the little boy, catching him on the back of the head. Then, with a quick jump North was at his side again, and had the little fellow's arm in a cruel grip.

"Try to run away from me; will you?" he demanded. "I'll show you that it won't do to fool with me—you prep. kids are getting too fresh. Now you get down on your knees and beg my pardon, and then take my glove and bat, and Mersfeld's bat too."

"Oh, North—" began the pitcher, who was a fairly decent chap.

"Let me manage him," exclaimed the bully. "These kids have to be taught their place. Get down on your bones, now!"

He seized the frail lad's hands in his strong ones, and bent them over backward.

"Oh, Mr. North! Please don't. I—I won't do it again! I'll carry the bat! Oh, you're breaking my hands!"

He cried out in agony, and Mersfeld took a step forward half intending to interfere. But he did not get the chance.

Some one with blazing eyes leaped from behind the clump of bushes and confronted the bully. A clenched fist was drawn back, and then shot forward. Right on the point of North's aristocratic chin it landed with a sound that could be heard for some distance.

Backward the bully was hurled, almost turning over, and then he slumped down on the grass. He stayed there for several seconds, and then got up slowly.

"Who—who did that?" he asked thickly, for he was a bit dazed.

"I did," answered Cap Smith quietly, "and if you want any additional just try some more of your bullying tactics on boys smaller than yourself."

North staggered to his feet, and rushed at Cap.

"Not here! Not now!" cried Mersfeld, throwing himself in front of his crony. "Meet him later! There'll have to be a fight, of course?" and the pitcher looked at Cap.

"Of course," was the grave answer.

"All right. I'll see one of your friends," for these matters were rather scientifically arranged at Westfield, on certain occasions.

"See Bill or Pete," answered Cap, as he turned aside and strolled up the campus.

CHAPTER XXIII

THE FIGHT

"T<small>IME</small>!"

It was the call of the watch-holder, and, as he spoke the word, two scantily clad figures leaped toward each other.

"Take him easy now, Cap!" cautioned Bill to his larger brother.

"Go in and finish him!" advised Mersfeld to North, for whom he was acting as second. Merton was keeping time, and Ward, the other Senior who had been the unbidden guest at the little spread was referee.

It was the fight between North and Cap Smith—the fight which was the inevitable outcome of the interference when the bully was mistreating little Harvey.

The contest took place where all such affairs were "pulled off," if I may use such a term, in a well-secluded spot back of the baseball grandstand.

"Watch his left!" was the further advice of Bill, who was acting as second, gave to his brother, while Mersfeld sarcastically cut in with:

"Look out for biting in the clinches, North."

It was a useless insult, for Cap never answered it.

Narrowly he watched his opponent, looking into his eyes, and trying to guess, by close observations of those organs, how the lead would be.

Out shot North's left, after a weak feint with his right. Cap was not deceived. Cleverly he blocked the blow and countered with his left. His aim was a bit short, but it caught North over the eye, too lightly to raise a mark, however.

Those Smith Boys on the Diamond

The fight was now on, and for a time blows were delivered with such rapidity that the onlookers were in doubt as to who was having the best of it. It was give and take, yet it was not brutal.

For the lads were both healthy and strong, and the soft gloves which the Seniors had insisted that they wear, precluded any serious damage to either. Nor were they scientific enough to do any material harm, for though they had both taken boxing lessons, they were far from being in the class with pugilists.

North half turned, made a feint as though to drive his right into Cap's face, quickly shifted, and shot out his left.

"Wow!" cried Mersfeld in anticipation of what was about to happen to the youth against whom he bore a grudge.

But it was the unexpected which took place, for North in making the shift had left himself unguarded for one fatal moment.

In shot the ready left of Cap Smith, straight from the shoulder, with all the steam behind it which our hero could muster, and North was neatly bowled over, bleeding slightly from the nose.

"First blood for us!" called Bill shrilly.

"Well, you needn't shout over it, and bring McNibb here!" grumbled Mersfeld, as he hurried to his fallen champion.

"I—I'm all right!" gasped North. "My—my foot slipped on the grass."

"Like fun!" retorted Pete. "You'll have some more of those 'slips' before it's over."

"That'll do," spoke Ward quietly. He looked at his classmate.

"Time," called Merton, for North had been attended by his second, while Bill looked after Cap, who was in no way distressed.

"Don't hurry to finish him," whispered Bill, as Cap arose from his knee to go forward. "You can do him."

"I don't know about that," was the cautious reply. "He has a strong right, and guards pretty well. I just managed to get in."

"Don't let him get you that way again," advised Mersfeld to his friend. "It's too risky."

"I won't, if I can help it."

They were at it again, hammer and tongs, giving and taking. Several body blows were exchanged, making both lads grunt, but doing no damage.

Then, when Cap tried for another left to the jaw he either miscalculated, or North guarded quickly, for Cap's fist came against his opponent's forearm, and the next minute our hero went down under a well directed blow, that eventually closed his right eye. But he did not mind this, got up quickly and was at it again.

Seeing his advantage in the next round North hammered away at Cap's optic, thereby not only causing the Smith lad exquisite pain, but greatly hampering him in the fight, for his vision was reduced by half.

"You've got him now!" exulted Mersfeld, when the round was over, and he was spraying his man with water from a ginger ale bottle. "Keep at him!"

"Oh, he's got lots of go yet," declared North. "If I can close his other eye I'll have him though."

"Then play for that."

North tried to, but he was so intent on this that he left his own chin unguarded. Cap did not care much about inflicting visible punishment on the bully, but he did want to end the fight, for which, truth to tell, he had no great hankering.

Once more his reliable left went boring in, and North gently went over backwards, coming heavily down in the grass. He almost took the count, but the time keeper was merciful, and allowed him a few seconds.

Those Smith Boys on the Diamond

"He's about all in," whispered Bill to his brother, when after some feeble and cautious sparring the round was at an end. "Finish him up. I'm afraid McNibb or some of the profs. might come."

"So am I. Here goes for a knock-out."

Cap tried for it, but North was shifty. He was playing on the defensive now, for he found that Cap was more cautious and was guarding his damaged eye well. And North did not dare open his guard enough to come back strong. Therefore he clinched several times, hanging heavily on his opponent to tire him.

Cap tried to avoid this, and there was considerable leg work which was hard on the breathing apparatus. He thought he saw one good chance, and sent in an upper cut, but it fell short, and he got a blow on the ear that made his head ring.

Thereafter he was more cautious.

"You must do him up soon," implored Bill. "Can't you take a chance?"

"I'm afraid to, with my bad eye."

"That's so. Well, use your own judgment."

But the next round was the last, and the end came most unexpectedly. North led with his right, intending to try once more his feinting, shifting tactics. But he made a miscalculation. Cap blocked with his left, and sending in a cross-counter with his right caught North on the side of the head.

Down went the bully like a log, not badly hurt, but stunned enough to make him take the count. There was no chance to allow the fatal ten seconds to elapse, however, for, from the crowd that surrounded the two contestants came the cry:

"Here comes Prexy!"

"Skip! Here's Dr. Burton!"

"Come on, Cap! Get into your coat—never mind your shirt—out this way!" cried Bill, Pete and Whistle-Breeches in the same breath.

Cap looked afar, and saw the figure of the venerable president bearing down on them. The head of Westfield school was eagerly perusing one book, and had another under his arm.

Cap hurriedly dressed as best he could. He saw North slowly rising, assisted by his friends. Cap started toward him.

"Where you going?" demanded Bill.

"To shake hands—it's all over. I want to be friends."

"You've no time. I doubt if we can get away as it is."

Bill, Pete, Whistle-Breeches and some of the others tried to get Cap in their midst, so that his blackened eye would not be seen. They hoped to be able to get back to their rooms by a round-about path, but, alas for their hopes. Dr. Burton looked up, saw them, and changing his course, bore down more directly on them.

"It's all up!" groaned Pete.

Bill looked around, and saw North and his friends hurrying into the dressing rooms under the grandstand. He wished he had thought of that, but there was no time now.

CHAPTER XXIV

THE KIDNAPPED PITCHER

"WHAT'LL you say when he asks you what's up?" asked Whistle-Breeches.

"Guess I'll have to tell the truth," answered Cap.

"Couldn't you say you ran into the fence catching a foul ball?" inquired Bill.

"Nothing doing," was his brother's retort. "The doctor would guess right in a minute. Besides, I wouldn't fake it that way."

"Of course not. I was only joking. Well, he'll be here in a second. He's looking at us as if undecided whether we were Greek roots or some Sanskrit characters. Maybe he'll pass us up," went on Bill.

"No such luck!" groaned Pete. "Pull your cap down farther over your eyes, and maybe he won't see the bruise."

But all the efforts of the lads were seemingly to go for naught. The venerable president, squinting at them through his thick spectacles, smiled in a friendly fashion, as he came nearer. The students halted and touched their caps.

"Ah, boys, just coming from a game?" inquired Dr. Burton.

"Yes, sir," answered Whistle-Breeches, who, being slightly taller than Cap, had stepped in front of him.

"Ah, and who won, may I ask?"

"We—er—that is we didn't finish," answered Bill, hoping to draw attention away from Cap.

"The season has opened well, I hope," went on the doctor. "And there are good chances for keeping the pennant here, I trust?"

"We're going to try hard," put in Pete, who, being on the other side, trusted to draw the attention of the president farther away from his brother. As for that hero he remained quiet.

"Pull your cap farther down!" again advised Bill in a hoarse whisper.

Whether it was that or whether he would have noticed it anyhow, the eyes of the president went straight to Cap's bruised countenance. He saw the blackened eye, and the cuts and scratches.

"Ah, there has been an accident, I see," he remarked, and he advanced closer to the lad.

"Er—yes—that is I—"

"Cut it out," whispered Bill, nudging his brother in the back.

"Hit by a ball, I suppose," went on the president. "And yet they say baseball is comparatively harmless. Why, you look almost as if you had been through a football scrimmage, Smith."

"Ye—yes, sir," stammered Cap.

"Better have it attended to right away," continued Dr. Burton. "That eye looks very painful."

"It is," murmured Cap.

"And you had better wear a stronger mask," were the doctor's parting words, as he turned aside. There was a queer smile on his face, and his eyes twinkled behind his glasses. He opened his book at the place where a cautious finger had kept the pages apart, and passed on.

"Talk about luck!" exclaimed Whistle-Breeches hoarsely. "He never even suspected that there'd been a fight. Oh, you Cap!"

"Suspected!" burst out Bill. "I'll bet he knows all about it!"

"He did not!" declared the other lad. "Why, he's so interested in that book that I don't believe he remembers now whether he spoke to us or not."

"He doesn't; eh?" exclaimed Bill. "Say, he went off reading his book upside down, and if that doesn't indicate that he's on to our game, and is laughing at our attempts to keep it from him, I'd like to know what it does mean?"

"Was his book upside down?"

"Surest thing you know. Say, what the doctor doesn't know wouldn't cover a postage stamp. But it was white of him not to let on. You're lucky, Cap!"

"Yes, regular Smith luck," put in Whistle-Breeches.

"Well, don't take any chances. Cut away to your room. I can get you some raw beefsteak for the optic."

"An oyster is better," declared Pete, and they scientifically discussed the various merits of the two.

"If we had Professor Clatter here he'd paint it with some eye dope and Cap would look all to the merry." suggested Bill. But the traveling medicine man was not available, and Cap had to do the best he could.

It was some days before he was decently presentable and North was just as bad. Of course the faculty must have suspected the reason for the darkened eyes and bruised faces, but as there was no official report or complaint, nothing was said of it, and the matter was dropped.

The upper classmen took up the question, and a sort of truce was patched up between Cap and the bully, but though North professed to be friendly there was a sullen look in his eyes, and Cap knew he would do him a bad turn if he got the chance. Mersfeld and North were thicker than ever, and the Smith boys agreed among themselves to be on their guard.

Meanwhile there was baseball a plenty. Some league games were played, and a number of minor contests took place. It was drawing close to the time for the annual Freshman battle on the diamond with Tuckerton, and this game was always a hotly contested one, and eagerly looked forward to by the first year students and their friends.

"We stand a better chance to win this time, than ever before," remarked Armitage, who was captain of the first year team. "We've got Bill to pitch, and he's a wonder."

The Varsity twirler did occupy the box for the Freshmen nine, and no objection had been raised to this arrangement until nearly time for the Tuckerton game. Then the nine of that school sent in a formal protest, objection to Bill on the ground that though a first year lad, he was not properly a member of the Freshman team, since he was the Varsity pitcher.

"Well, we'll just ignore that objection, and if they don't want to play with Bill in the box we'll claim the game by forfeit," decided Armitage. The dispute waxed hot and an appeal was taken to the student body which governed athletics among the members of the school league. They decided that Bill could pitch.

"Well, he won't if we fellows have any spunk," declared Borden, the Tuckerton captain.

"Spunk? How do you mean?" asked Swain, the pitcher.

"I mean that we can put up a game on him so that he can't pitch against us, and they'll have to put in Potter, the substitute. We can knock *him* out of the box, but Bill Smith is no easy mark. It means losing the game for us to bat against Bill."

"But what can we do?" asked Swain.

"Get Bill out of the way the day before the game."

"How?"

"Kidnap him, of course. Spirit him away, and keep him in cold storage until we win. Are you game?"

"Can it be done?" asked Swain.

"Of course. I'll arrange it, if you fellows will help."

Those Smith Boys on the Diamond

"Certainly we will, but how is it to be done?"

"Easy enough. We'll just meet him in the dark on the road, bundle him into my auto, and take him to a quiet place where he can't get away." Borden was a rich youth, and had an automobile which he had brought to school with him.

He went more into detail about his plan, and after realizing that it would mean losing the game if Bill pitched against them, his teammates somewhat reluctantly agreed to the scheme. They thought they were within their rights for they totally disagreed with the finding of the governing body that Bill was entitled to pitch as a Freshman, even though he was on the Varsity.

"Suppose they find out we did it, and take the game from us even after we win?" suggested Cadmus, who was the Tuckerton Freshman catcher.

"They'll never discover it," boasted Borden. "They'll lay it to some of the Sophs or Juniors at Westfield, and Bill will never recognize us for we'll wear masks."

"All right, we're with you," decided his chums. "Now for the details."

These were soon settled. It was agreed that Bill should be captured the night before the game, when there would be little chance that he could be rescued in time to play.

"But how will we get hold of him," asked Cadmus.

"I'll send him some sort of a message," replied Borden. "I'll write a note, in a disguised hand, and ask him to call at a certain place in the village. We'll be on the lookout and when he goes past that lonely stretch of woods, on the main road we'll grab him, run him off in my car to a place I know of, and leave him there."

"Suppose some of his brothers or friends come with him?" Swain wanted to know.

"Oh, well, we can get away with Bill before they realize what's up. You fellows want everything too easy."

When, on the night before the game with Tuckerton, Bill Smith received a note, asking him to call at a certain hotel in the village, there to talk over baseball matters, the pitcher showed the missive to his brothers.

"Looks sort of fishy," decided Cap.

"What name is signed to it?" inquired Pete.

"Just says 'Baseball Crank,'" was the reply. "I think it's a joke."

"Are you going?" asked Whistle-Breeches.

"Might as well. But I'm going to go easy, and take a look around before I go inside. Maybe I can turn the tables."

"Tell you what we'll do," broke in Cap.

"What?"

"We'll all go with Bill. Then, if there's any trouble we can help him. Maybe North or Mersfeld put up this game."

"That's right," agreed Bill. "I'll be glad if you fellows will come along, though it may be straight after all."

So, after obtaining from the proctor permission to go to the village on condition that they would be back before locking-up time, the three Smith brothers, and Whistle-Breeches sallied forth. They never suspected there might be a joke perpetrated on them while on their way, rather expecting some game in the village, and so proceeded along the highway in careless ease, singing and joking.

As they reached a lonely stretch of woods, just below getting into the village, three figures sprang out from the underbrush. Over their faces were strips of cloth, and at the first sight of the trio our friends drew back in some alarm, feeling they had met with a gang of highwaymen.

"That's the one—in the centre!" called a hoarse voice, and a grab was made for Bill. Before his brothers or Whistle-Breeches could rally to his aid he was borne off, struggling and kicking against his unknown captors.

"Into the car with him—quick!" was the whispered order, and, ere the three lads left standing in the road had recovered from their astonishment, there sounded the chug-chug of an automobile, and Bill was whisked away.

"Well, wouldn't that get your goat!" gasped Cap, as he stood looking at the fast-disappearing red tail lamp of the machine. "They've got Bill!"

"Come on after 'em!" yelled Pete, starting down the highway on a run. "We've got to rescue him!"

CHAPTER XXV

TO THE RESCUE

"Here! Come back!" cried Cap.

"What for?" demanded Pete, pausing in the darkness, and gazing first toward the disappearing red light and then toward where his brother stood.

"You can't catch an auto, no matter if you are a good base runner," replied the older Smith lad. "Come here."

"That's right, I guess there isn't much use running," admitted Pete dubiously, as he slowly returned.

"But they've got Bill, and we ought to help him. Maybe they'll hold him for a ransom."

"It's only a joke," decided Cap. "Come on, we've got to use our brains against these fellows, and maybe we can turn the tables on them. First we'll go on to town, and see if any of them really are at the hotel. We may get a line on them there."

But there was no trace of any one at the hostelry who might, by any stretch of the imagination, be considered as of those who had a part in the kidnapping.

"Back to school," ordered Cap. "We'll see if there's anything doing there."

It did not take long to learn that no hazing was going on that night, and that none of the various school societies were engaged in any pranks, and when it was made clear that neither Mersfeld nor North had been out of their rooms, they were absolved from the half-suspicion that pointed to them.

"But Bill's gone," said Pete blankly.

"Yes, and it's up to us to find him," decided Cap. "I guess to-morrow—"

"By Jove, to-morrow is the date for the big Freshman game with Tuckerton!" exclaimed Whistle-Breeches. "You know how they protested against him. I'll bet a cookie, without a hole in it, that—"

"Say no more!" burst out Bob Chapin, with a tragic gesture. "The plot is laid bare! Tuckerton has our hero! On to the rescue!"

But it was too late to do anything that night, though probably had the college authorities been appealed to they would have permitted further search. However our friends preferred to work out the problem themselves.

Meanwhile poor Bill was being rapidly carried away, whither he knew not. All that he was aware of was that a cloth had been wound around his head and face to prevent him from seeing or from crying out. Then he was bundled into an auto, and the car was speeded up.

Bill tried to listen and catch any sounds that might indicate where he was being taken, but Borden, who wanted to make speed had the muffler cut out and the only noise the pitcher heard was that made by the machine.

It was a rough road over which he was being taken, and the car swayed and pitched from side to side, tossing Bill about. When he first felt himself grabbed by his unknown assailants he had tried to struggle away from them, but they had skilfully wound ropes about his legs and arms, and now, bundled up as he was in one corner of the gasoline vehicle, he tried in vain to free himself. But the ropes held.

At length, however, lack of air, by reason of the cloth being too tightly drawn over his head, caused the unlucky lad to give utterance to a muffled appeal.

"I say, you fellows don't want me to smother; do you?" he demanded.

"No, of course not," came the cool answer. "If you'll promise not to make a row we'll take off some of the horse blankets. How about it?"

Bill listened intently. He did not recognize the voice. He was minded to return a fierce answer, that he would suit himself about calling for help, but he recalled that in many cases discretion is the better part of valor. So, rather meekly, he made answer:

"I'll be good, kind Mr. Highwayman!"

There was a stifled laugh at this.

"Takes it well," remarked one of his captors in a whisper.

"Yes—but wait," was the significant comment. "You take off some of the wrappings. Be careful he doesn't spot you."

Bill was soon more comfortable, as far as breathing was concerned, but his limbs were still cramped from the cords that bound them, and he was in a most uncomfortable position. He seemed to be reclining in the tonneau of the car, and some one was in the seat with him. He tried his best to make out the features, but it was dark, and the half masks which his captors wore prevented recognition.

Nor did the voices afford any clew, for when those in the auto spoke it was either in half whispers or in mumbled words so that the tones were not clear. At first Bill thought it was some of the students from Westfield who were playing a joke on him, but later he changed this opinion. He had an idea that it was either Mersfeld, North or some of their crowd, but the conversation among his captors soon disclosed that they were not these lads.

"I wonder what they want of me, anyhow," mused Bill. "It was foolish to pay any attention to that note. I wish I had looked more carefully at the writing."

Yet, as he tried to recall the characters he was sure he had never seen the hand before.

"It's a joke, though, sure," decided the pitcher. "And it's some young fellows who have me in tow. Guess I'll talk and see if they'll answer."

He squirmed into an easier position, and fired this question at those in the auto:

"Where are you taking me?"

"You'll soon see," was the reply.

"If I ever find out who you are, I'll pay you back well for this," went on Bill.

"You're welcome to—if you find out," was the significant answer.

"I know you!" suddenly exclaimed the captive. "You're fellows from Sandrim, trying to get even for us boys taking your boats," went on Bill, for, not long before that, the lads from Westfield had carried a lot of boats from their rival school, and deposited the craft in the middle of their own campus. "You're from Sandrim," declared Bill positively.

A laugh was his only answer. The auto kept up the speed, and presently turned from the main road, into a sort of lane.

"Is this the place?" asked the lad who was in the tonneau with Bill.

"A little farther," answered the one at the wheel. "Look out he doesn't slip away from you."

"Oh, I've got him," was the reply, and a hand took a firmer grip of Bill's shoulder.

The car came to a sudden stop. A door of a building which the pitcher could see was a sort of shack, or hut, was opened, and a shaft of light came out.

"Is that you—" began a voice.

"Yes, keep quiet!" was the quick retort. "We've got him. Help carry him to the room, and don't talk."

Before Bill could prevent it he was again tied up, and some one lifted him from the car. He was carried along in the darkness, trying in vain to make out what sort of a place he was in.

Then he was laid, none too gently, on a pile of some rags in a corner of a dark room. The door was closed and Bill was left alone with his anxious and gloomy thoughts.

"Potato salad!" he gasped, half aloud, for the rags had been removed from around his head, "I hope I get away from here in time to play in the Freshman game to-morrow! It will be fierce if I don't."

Bill listened. He could hear the auto puffing away. He was left alone in the deserted shack—at least he thought he was alone, for he heard no noise.

Bright and early the next morning Pete and Cap were up, ready to go to the rescue of their brother. They arranged to cut their lectures that day, as did also Whistle-Breeches, and, though many more students wanted to take part in the search, it was thought best not to make too much of the affair.

"For, whoever has done it will hear about us getting excited about it and they'll have more of a laugh on us than ever," declared Cap. "It's a disgrace that we ever let Bill be captured."

"We couldn't help it," was Pete's opinion. "But we'll get him back."

Their first move in the morning was to go to the place where the kidnapping had occurred. There they saw the marks of some auto wheels, but, as several cars had passed by in the meanwhile it was impossible to do any tracing.

"We've got to make inquiries," decided Cap. "We'll ask along the road, of farmers and the people we meet."

They did not have much success for they could not describe the auto, nor those in it, and many cars had gone over the road.

"It's my notion that you're lookin' fer a needle in the haystack," was the opinion of one farmer whom they asked, and when the boys thought of it, they nearly agreed with him.

"But what will we do at the game if he doesn't show up?" demanded Captain Armitage. "It will be fierce to go up against Tuckerton without Bill in the box."

Those Smith Boys on the Diamond

"What *can* we do?" asked Pete hopelessly when a good part of the morning had gone, and there was no trace of the missing pitcher.

"Go right to Tuckerton, and accuse them!" suggested the irate captain. "Tell them we know they spirited Bill off, and demand that they produce him, or we'll not play."

"They'd laugh at us," said Cap. "Call us kindergartners, and all that sort of thing. No, we can't crawl that way. But I believe the Tuckerton fellows *did* have a hand in the game, and if we can only find out which of them hired an auto I think we'd have a clew."

"Maybe one of them owns a car," suggested Whistle-Breeches. It was a new thought for the searchers, and it was received joyously.

"By Jinks! That's the stuff!" cried Cap. "Pete, you get on that trail, and I'll inquire at the only garage in town if any of the fellows from Tuckerton hired a gasoline gig there. I'll meet you at the cross roads."

This was a place about half-way between the two schools which were only a few miles apart.

With Pete went Whistle-Breeches, to help in the inquiry, and Bob Chapin accompanied Cap. Meanwhile Captain Armitage was in despair, for he had counted on Bill to win the biggest part of the game, and without him he was sure his nine would lose. On the other hand there was rejoicing in the Tuckerton camp, when it was known that Bill was missing, though only a few of the members of the nine and its supporters, guessed the cause of his absence.

Noon came, and Bill was still among the missing. Cap had obtained no news at the town garage, and though Pete had learned that Borden of Tuckerton, owned a car, he could not locate that youth or his machine. For the nine had some grounds a distance from the school to practice before the big game.

"I guess it's no use," said Cap despairingly. "It's a queer sort of a joke, if that's what it is, and it looks as if Bill would be out of the game. You'll have to play without him, Armitage."

"Well, I'll wait until the last minute," decided the captain. "He may get away and join us. Lucky it's on our own grounds. We'll have that advantage. Poor Bill. I wonder where he is?"

CHAPTER XXVI

JUST IN TIME

BILL SMITH, about that same time, was wondering the same thing. He had dozed off after his captors had left him, but, with the first glint of morning sun into the room where he was a prisoner he had awakened. He was still bound.

"Well, this is pretty punk!" he exclaimed. "To think that they got ahead of me this way! I wonder where I am, anyhow? And I wonder how I can get away, and back—Great muskmelons! If I don't show up at the game—"

The thought was too much for Bill. He resolved on bold tactics. Considering that his promise not to make an outcry ended with the leaving of his captors, he raised his voice in a shout.

"Help! Come here, somebody! Let me out! Police!"

Bill didn't particularly want the police, for he knew that his captivity was the result of some school prank, and the boys never called on the officers of the law if they could help it. But "Police!" was an easy word to say, and it carried well. Therefore the captive yelled it again and again.

But there was no answer to his cries, and after straining his throat until it ached, the pitcher decided that he had better save his breath and try other means to escape.

"First to see if I can't get rid of some of these ropes on my arms and legs," he murmured. He tugged and strained at them, after wiggling to a sitting position, but the knots had been made with care, and held. Bill tried to pull his hands from the loops but it was useless, and his feet were equally secure. He could not gnaw through the ropes as he had sometimes read of prisoners doing, for his hands were tied behind his back.

"I certainly am up against it," he said aloud. Then, for the first time, he took note of his prison. He was in a vacant room, evidently in some old fashioned house, to judge by the character of the woodwork and the wall paper. There were two windows, and a door, the latter apparently quite solid.

"Let's have a look outside," suggested Bill to himself. He struggled to his feet, and, by a series of hops, gained the windows. He was in the third story of a house, set in the midst of a neglected garden, and the scene that met the lad's gaze was unfamiliar to him.

"I might be a hundred miles from nowhere, for all I can tell," he concluded dubiously. "Well, now for a try at the door."

Hopping over to the portal Bill turned around with his back to it, and managed to reach the knob with his hands. It turned, but the door was locked.

"Nothing doing there!" exclaimed the captive. "Well, here's for some more noise." He yelled and shouted at the top of his voice, accompanying himself by beating on the door with his bound fists. Silence was his only answer.

Once more Bill hopped to the window. He looked out, hoping he might see some one to whom he could appeal. Then, as he gazed helplessly out, he noted a nail driven into one side of the casement. At once a plan came into his mind.

"If I can rub the rope that binds my hands, up and down over the head of that nail, I may fray the ropes enough to break them," he remarked aloud, for it made it seem less lonesome to speak thus. "Once I get my hands loose—" Bill did not finish, but he had great hopes of what he could then do.

He began at once with the rusty nail as a knife. It was hard work, and several times his hands slipped and his wrists were scratched, but he kept at it, and finally found that the cords were giving way. He worked faster, and then, with a sudden strain he found his arms free. Then it was an easy matter to loosen his feet, and he stood up unbound.

"Now for a try at that door!" exclaimed the lad, and after giving the knob a vigorous turn, and vainly pulling on the portal he began to kick it violently.

He was engaged in this, at the same time yelling and demanding to be released, when the door suddenly opened. So suddenly in fact that Bill toppled outward with it, and was caught in the arms of a big man who entered quickly, carrying the captive backward with him, and immediately locking the portal again.

Surprise bereft the lad of speech for a moment, and the man, after gazing at him, and noting the ropes on the floor, remarked:

"Well, you got rid of 'em yourself, I see. If you'd have waited a little longer I'd have taken 'em off. I'm a little late getting here with your breakfast."

"Breakfast!" gasped Bill. "You'd have taken off the ropes! Say, what kind of a game am I up against, anyhow?"

"Oh, I guess it's all right," said the man easily.

"Well it isn't all right," declared Bill. "If you don't let me out of here right away there's going to be the biggest row you ever saw," and, as if in support of his assertion the pitcher rushed over and began kicking on the door again.

"Hum! Them fellers was right," murmured the man seemingly not a bit disturbed by what Bill was doing.

"What fellows?" demanded the pitcher, pausing in his attack.

"The ones what brought you here. They said you'd cut up rough, and make a lot of fuss, an' by gum, they was right! I guess you sure enough do need a straight-jacket."

"A straight-jacket!" gasped poor Bill. "Say, for the love of cats, tell me what I'm up against; won't you?"

"I don't know, I'm sure," was the calm reply. "I was told to humor you until the keeper come, an' I'm doin' it. What would you like for breakfast?"

"I don't want any—let me out!" pleaded Bill. He was beginning to see the joke now.

"I don't dast," replied the man. "The fellers what brung you here said you was dangerous at times, an' I might be held responsible. They fetched you here in an automobile, an' arranged with me to leave you in this vacant house of mine until they could come again, with keepers from the lunatic asylum, to take you away. I'm expectin' 'em every minute, but they said I was to untie you by daylight, an' feed you, as you was less violent when it wasn't dark."

"Say, look here!" cried Bill. "Do you think I'm crazy?"

"I'm sure of it," was the answer. "At least, no, I ain't neither. There I clean forgot to say what them fellers told me to. No you ain't crazy. I am, an' everybody else is, but you're sane. That's what they said I was to tell you, if you asked me that question. All crazy persons thinks they are sane," he went on in explanation. "You're sane."

"But look here!" pleaded the captive. "Of course I'm sane. I'm a student at Westfield, and the fellows who brought me are either students from there, or from some other school, playing a joke on me. Now let me go!"

The man shook his head.

"They told me you'd say that, too," he said. "I can't let you go. I promised to keep you here until the keepers came, an' I'm goin' to do it. Now take it easy and you'll be all right. I'll bring you some breakfast. You look hungry."

"I am, but say—" Then the hopelessness of appealing any further to the man came forcibly to Bill, and he was silent.

"That's better," announced the man, preparing to unlock the door again. "I live over here a little way. This house belongs to me, but it's been vacant some time, so you can yell and holler all you please—no one will hear you. I'll go get you some victuals. Is there anything special you'd like? My wife is a good cook."

"Oh, bring anything," said poor Bill. He knew that he would have to eat if he was to keep up his strength, for he had determined to try to escape by the windows as soon as he was left alone again. He had a wild idea of making a rush when the farmer opened the door, but a look at the bulky frame of the man made him change his mind.

The food was good and Bill ate a hearty meal. Then he was left alone again, the farmer, on locking the door, saying that he expected the keepers any moment. It was evident that he believed the stories the captors of Bill had told him.

Once he was alone, and when a look from the windows had assured him that he was not being watched, Bill began to put into operation his plan of getting away.

He hoped that the ropes which had bound him would enable him to make his way down them out of the window, but on tying the pieces together he discovered that they were not long enough.

"Up against it!" exclaimed the lad, until, looking more carefully out of the end casement he discovered that a stout lightning rod ran near it, down the side of the house.

"That's just the cheese, if it will hold me," murmured the lad. "I'm going to try it anyhow."

He crawled out on the window sill, tested the rod as best he could, and then swung himself down it. To his joy it held, and in a few seconds he was safe on the ground.

"Now to find out where I am, and streak it for school and the game!" he murmured, looking around to see that the farmer was not in sight. He got his bearings and was soon out on a dusty highway. He ran for some distance until a turn in the road hid the house of his captivity from him, and then slowed down to a walk.

The surroundings were still unfamiliar to him, but meeting a man driving a carriage he learned that he was near the village of Belleville, about twenty miles from Westfield.

"And it's coming on noon, I haven't half enough to buy a railroad ticket, and the game is called at two o'clock!" groaned Bill. "I certainly am up against it good and hard!"

The man whom he had accosted was going in the wrong direction, or he would have given the lad a lift. However, he did consent to drive him to the railroad station.

"I'll see if I can't give the agent a hard-luck story, and have him trust me for a ticket," thought the pitcher.

But the station agent proved to be a hard-featured man, who had once lost a dollar by lending it to a young lady who told him a pathetic story, and he turned a deaf ear to Bill's pleading.

"No money no ticket," he declared.

"But look here," gasped Bill. "Some fellows, either at my school, or from Tuckerton, played a joke on me last night—kidnapped me. I'm to pitch in the championship Freshman baseball game at two o'clock this afternoon, and I've just *got* to be there. I'll pay you back if you trust me for a ticket. Or say, you can ship me as express, C. O. D. and the boys will pay the charges at Westfield."

"Live stock has to travel in cattle cars, not as express," answered the agent with a grim smile. "Besides I don't believe in baseball anyhow. Some boys was battin' a ball once, an' they busted one of the windows in this ticket office. I had to pay for it, too! I ain't got no manner of likin' for baseball."

Bill saw that it was no use in pleading, and turned away. With despair in his heart he noted that it was nearly one o'clock. He might as well give up. Already the players were beginning to get ready for the game. In fancy he could hear the words of wonder at his absence from the diamond.

"They may think I threw the game," thought Bill, and then he remembered that his brothers and Whistle-Breeches had seen him captured, and would tell the story.

"They'd come to the rescue if they only knew where to come, too," thought Bill gloomily.

The pitcher was in desperate straits. A search through his pockets disclosed the fact that he had nothing to pawn on which to raise money, even if there had been a pawn shop in the village. He was just giving up, deciding to walk to Westfield, hoping to arrive before dark, when, as he left the station he nearly collided with a pretty girl, who was just entering, having alighted from a trim little motor car, that was still puffing outside.

"I beg your pardon," mumbled Bill.

"Oh!" exclaimed the girl. "I—why it's Mr. Smith!" she cried, holding out her hand. "I'm glad to meet you again. But why aren't you over at school at the big game? I'm on my way there."

For a moment you could have knocked Bill down with the wind from a slow ball, as he afterward expressed it. He looked at the girl, and recognized her as Miss Ruth Morton, to whom he had been introduced by Bob Chapin at one of the school games.

"Miss Morton!" he murmured. "I—Oh, if you're going to Westfield will you take me? I'm marooned!"

Then, rapidly, he blurted out the whole story of his capture and his inability to get back.

"Take you! Of course I'll take you!" exclaimed Miss Morton. "I have to stop for a girl friend, who is going to the game with me, but there'll be plenty of room for you."

"I'll ride on the mud guard or hang on back!" exclaimed Bill, a gleam of hope lighting his woe-begone countenance. "Only I want to beat Tuckerton!"

"And I want you to, even if a—a friend of mine goes there. I think it was an awfully mean trick they played on you."

"Oh, I'm not *sure* any Tuckerton fellows did it," said Bill, who wanted to play fair. "It may have been some of the Westfield crowd," but he had his own opinion.

Miss Morton, who had come to the station to inquire about some express package, hurried out to her car, followed by Bill. He offered to run it for her, but she was not a little proud of her own ability to drive.

"We've got to make time," suggested the pitcher nervously.

"I can do it," the girl assured him, and, once she had thrown in the third gear, the pitcher had no reason to complain of lack of speed.

Miss Morton's girl friend—Miss Hazel Dunning—was taken aboard and then, with Bill sitting on the floor in front, and resting his feet on the mud-guard step, for the machine was only a runabout, the trip to Westfield was begun.

Back on the school diamond there was an anxious throng of students and players. The news of Bill's kidnapping was known all over, and while there was despair in the ranks of the Westfield Freshmen and their supporters, there was ill-concealed joy among the Tuckerton nine and their adherents.

"Those fellows know where Bill is," declared Cap.

"But we don't dare accuse them," agreed Pete.

"And we'll lose the game," went on Armitage dubiously.

Bill never forgot his trip with Miss Morton. She was a daring driver, for a girl, and once or twice took chances that made even the nerve-hardened pitcher wince. But with a merry laugh she sped on, after cutting in ahead of a load of hay, on a narrow bridge.

Once there was a hail from a speed-watching constable but the girl kept on.

"There's oil on my number, and I never expect to come this way again," she declared recklessly.

"If only we don't get a blow-out!" murmured Miss Dunning.

"Don't you dare suggest such a thing, Hazel!" cried Miss Morton.

She turned on more speed. It lacked five minutes to two, and Bill knew the game would be called on the dot. They were two miles away, and could hardly get there on time, but the pitcher consoled himself with the reflection that at least he could take part after the first inning.

"Are we going to make it?" asked Miss Dunning.

"We've *got* to!" declared Miss Morton, as she swung around in front of a farm wagon, thereby causing the grizzled driver symptoms of heart failure.

Bill could hear the shouts on the diamond now. He was in a fever of excitement, and stood up to catch a first glimpse of the field. Miss Morton, with her lips set firmly around her pretty mouth grasped the steering wheel more rigidly and drove on. Toward the diamond she turned. There was another cheer from the crowd, but Bill could not see what was going on, and feared the game had started. There came a break in the throng and he had a glimpse of the field. What he saw reassured him.

"I'm just in time!" he gasped. "They're only practicing!"

He leaped out as the girl brought the car to a sudden stop with both brakes grinding and screeching.

"See you later! A thousand thanks—never could have done it but for you, Miss Morton!" burst out Bill as he ran over the grass. "I'll never forget it."

"Me either," murmured the girl. "I never drove so fast before in all my life, but I wasn't going to tell him so," she confided to her chum, as they left the car and walked toward the grand stand.

CHAPTER XXVII

A SCRIMMAGE

"PLAY ball!" called the umpire.

"Wait! Wait!" begged Bill breathlessly, as he ran forward. "I'm in time! I can play. Where's Armitage? I've been locked up—couldn't get here before! Can't I play?"

A cheer greeted Bill's unexpected appearance. His brothers who had given up hope rushed forward to clap him on the back. Whistle-Breeches did a war dance around him. There was wild rejoicing among the Westfield Freshmen. The Tuckerton Freshmen looked glum.

"Well, he got here after all," muttered Swain, the pitcher, to Captain Borden.

"Yes. That farmer must have let him go before I meant him to."

"What are you going to do—protest again?" asked Cadmus.

"No; what's the use? I think they're suspicious as it is. All we can do now is to play to beat 'em. Hang the luck anyhow, but—I s'pose it serves us right." Borden had the grace to admit that much.

Meanwhile Bill had rapidly told the story of his captivity and his ride in the auto.

"I tell you what we ought to do!" declared Armitage angrily, "we ought to refuse to play them, and claim the game. The idea of kidnapping our pitcher!"

"Easy!" exclaimed Cap.

"That's right," put in Bill. "I wasn't hurt any, and it was rather a lark after I got away. Besides we don't know for sure that Borden and his crowd did it, though I'm almost positive it was his auto. But never mind. Let's play ball."

"It's too late to get into uniform," remarked the captain, "and we're to take the field."

"I'll pitch as I am, and borrow a uniform when it's our turn to bat," spoke Bill.

"But can you twirl?" inquired his brother. "After what you've been through—away all night—knocked around in an auto, no decent meal—"

"That's where you're wrong, I had one good meal, and the next one can wait until we win the game. Miss Morton—she's several kinds of a pretty brick, by the way—she got some sandwiches on the trip in. My! She's a stunner! How she did drive! She—"

"Oh, get in your box, and play ball," interrupted Armitage, with a laugh at Bill's enthusiasm.

There were dubious looks on the faces of the Tuckerton players at the advent of the talented pitcher, but a gleam of hope came when Borden whispered that he might be all out of condition from his captivity, and could not hold his own in the box.

Curiously enough it did not occur to any of the conspiring rivals of Westfield that they had taken an unfair advantage in spiriting Bill away. They felt that he had no right, as the Varsity pitcher, to play with the Freshmen against them.

But if they hoped that Bill was out of condition they were doomed to disappointment, for when he had put on his glasses, which Cap had brought with him on a forlorn chance, Bill never pitched better ball. At first he was a little stiff, and issued several passes, whereat there was rejoicing among the visitors, and grim despair in the ranks of the home team. But Bill shook off his momentary indisposition, and when the final inning had ended in a dazzling succession of plays, the Westfield team had won by a score of ten runs to three.

"Wow, Oh, wow!" cried Armitage, hugging Bill. "If you hadn't come along we'd have been in the soup!"

"Nonsense!" objected Bill.

"It's true," said Whistle-Breeches. "Swain was in great form to-day."

"But Bill was better," added Pete.

"You could make a story out of what you went through," drawled Bob Chapin. "Ring in Miss Morton as the heroine."

"Only for her I'd never have made it," agreed Bill, as he went over to shake hands with the pretty, blushing girl.

"Oh, it was fine! Fine!" cried Miss Morton, as she greeted Bill and his companions who surrounded her and Miss Dunning.

"Perfectly wonderful the way you struck out the last three men," went on the other girl.

Bill blushed behind his ears. He was too tanned to have the color show elsewhere.

And so the Tuckerton-Westfield Freshmen game passed into school history, and Bill never really found out who had kidnapped him. In fact he never tried, for he concluded that his suspicions were good enough, and he did not want revenge.

The summer crept on, and the close of the term was near at hand. More games were played, and Westfield was doing well. She did not have, as yet by any means, a clear title to the pennant. In fact the loss of a few games would mean that Tuckerton or Sandrim would get it, but the Smith boys and their chums were working hard.

As for Mersfeld he was still under the ban, for when he was allowed to resume athletics he had gone so stale that after a try-out he was relegated to the ranks of the subs for the Varsity, and Bill's place as first pitcher was undisputed. And there was bitterness in the heart of the former twirler.

"Oh, if I could only get square with him!" he muttered to North.

"There's only one way to put him out of the running," declared that worthy.

"And that is—?"

"To get his special glasses. He can't get another pair made in time now, for that old codger of an astronomer has been arrested I hear, and the other professor hasn't been around lately. There's only a week more before the close of the season, and if you get the specks Bill couldn't pitch. You might have a chance then."

"I wish we could get 'em, but we risked it once, and—"

"We'll have to do it differently this time. No more trying to sneak into his room. We've got to take the glasses away from him personally."

"How? Hold him up some dark night? That won't do, for he only carries them with him going to and from the games."

"And that's just when I mean to take them. If we could get him into what would look like a friendly scrimmage say, one of us could frisk the glasses out of his pocket, and he'd be left when he tried to pitch next time."

"Can it be done?"

"Sure. If you're with me just hang around the next time Bill comes off the diamond. I'll start something, you come back at me, we'll run around Bill and his brothers—maybe upset 'em, and in the confusion if I can't get the glasses I'm no good. I know where he carries 'em."

"All right, North. If I can only get back on the team I'd do anything!"

"Then it's settled," was the reply, and the two cronies walked away together, talking of their mean plot.

Their chance came the next day, when a crowd of the players were returning from the ball field after a practice game.

"Tag, you're it!" suddenly cried North to Mersfeld, and he began circling about Bill, Pete and Cap, who were walking with Whistle-Breeches.

"Oh, cut it out!" cried Mersfeld, as if in objection, and he tripped North up. The latter in falling made a grab for Bill, as if to save himself, and in an instant the two went down in a heap and there was a laughing, struggling crowd of youths rolling over the grass in what was apparently a friendly scrimmage.

CHAPTER XXVIII

THE GLASSES ARE GONE

"Here get up off me, can't you?" demanded Bill, as he found himself under North's no light weight. The latter had his arms around the pitcher.

"Sorry. Did I hurt you?" asked the bully with elaborate politeness as he helped Bill to his feet.

"No, but I don't want my nose rubbed in the dirt. It might spoil the shape."

"That's right. Wait until I get hold of Mersfeld. It was his fault."

North scurried off, pretending to be in pursuit of his crony, while Cap, Pete and Whistle-Breeches, who had gone down in the melee were fighting off several of their chums who, seeing the prostrate group, had, boy fashion, thrown themselves on top, a-la-football practice.

"Oh, say, this is too much!" gasped Cap, as he tossed Bob Chapin to one side.

"Yes, who started this, anyhow?" demanded Pete, digging some grass out of his left ear.

The skirmishing and fun were general now, and no one seemed to remember that Mersfeld and North had been the storm centre. The two were far enough away, over the campus by this time.

"Well, did you get 'em?" asked Mersfeld nervously, as he looked back at the throng of lads who had ceased their struggles and were brushing what they could of the dirt off their clothes.

"I sure did," was the answer. "Look," and he showed him a small black case, which, on being opened, disclosed the peculiar glasses that Bill wore when he pitched.

"Good!" exclaimed the deposed pitcher. "Now what'll we do with 'em?"

"Here, you take 'em," and North held them out.

"Not much!" came the quick answer.

"Why not?"

"Think I want to be caught with them on me?"

"Well, I don't want 'em either. Shall I throw 'em away?" and he made a half-motion toward a clump of bushes.

"No, some one might find 'em, and give 'em back, and then we'd be as badly off as before. Here, I'll tell you what to do. Toss 'em into that old cannon," and Mersfeld pointed to one on the far edge of the campus. It was a Spanish war trophy, loaned by the government. "No one will ever think of looking there for 'em."

With a quick motion North slid the case of spectacles down the muzzle. Then the two quickly kept on their way.

Bill and his friends proceeded to the gymnasium, where the players indulged in a shower bath, and, a little later the three brothers were in Cap's room, talking over baseball matters in particular, and everything in general.

"Let's see," mused the pitcher as he looked over a schedule of dates. "We play Northampton day after to-morrow, Sandrim the next day, and then Saturday winds up the season with Tuckerton. And say, fellows, do you know we've got to win every game to keep the pennant!"

"How's that?" demanded Cap. "I thought we had a good lead?"

"So we did have, but Tuckerton and Sandrim have pulled up on us, and it's almost a tie now. Yes, we've got to make a clean sweep from now on or we'll not be in it."

"Well, we can do it," declared Pete vigorously.

"Sure," asserted Whistle-Breeches, as if it was the most simple thing in the world.

"Oh, certainly, my lords and gentlemen," added Bob Chapin half-mockingly. "Just sit here and figure it out by averages and percentages."

"Dry up!" advised Cap. "How's your arm holding out, Bill?"

"Oh, I guess I'll manage, though we're going to have a grandstand finish this week."

"How about your eyes," asked Whistle-Breeches. "Can't you get along without the glasses yet, Bill? I'm always afraid a ball will crack into them, and then you *would* be out of it."

"That part never worries me," said Bill. "I'm so used to 'em now that I'd feel lost in the box without 'em. They certainly were a great thing, and I—"

He paused suddenly, and hurriedly crossed the room to where his uniform was picturesquely draped over a chair. Rapidly the pitcher felt through the pockets, and a look of alarm came over his face. He began tossing aside a multitudinous collection of articles on his bureau.

"What's up, something bite you?" asked Pete.

Bill did not answer. He was feeling now in the pockets of the suit he wore. As he went from one to the other his face assumed a more and more worried look.

"For cats' sake what is it?" demanded Cap. "Lost a love letter? We won't read it if we find it."

"My glasses!" gasped Bill.

"Your glasses?" repeated Whistle-Breeches.

"Yes—they're gone," and with a wild look on his face the pitcher dashed from the room and ran toward the gymnasium, followed by his brothers.

CHAPTER XXIX

MERSFELD IN THE BOX

THERE was a wild search in and about the gymnasium on the part of Bill, his brothers and his chums, but of course the missing glasses were not found.

"Are you sure you dropped them here?" asked Cap, as he went over again the room which his brother had used as a dressing department before and after the shower bath.

"Well, I'm not sure, of course," answered Bill, "but they're gone, and I must have dropped them somewhere."

They went over the place inch by inch, looked in odd nooks and corners and inquired of the janitors and helpers, but the spectacles were not found.

"Say," cried Whistle-Breeches with sudden illumination, "I'll bet you dropped them that time we were all fooling on the campus!"

"By Jinks! I believe I did!" cried Bill, and he made a mad dash for the place. The others followed and soon the lads were scanning the grass, going about on their hands and knees. From a vantage point Mersfeld and North watched.

"He's missed 'em all right," exulted the deposed pitcher.

"Sure, and he'll look a good while for 'em, too."

"Think he'll suspect us?"

"Not a bit of it," replied North. He started toward the group of searching lads.

"Here! Where are you going?" cried his companion in alarm.

"Going over to help 'em hunt."

"Come back! Do you want to give the whole thing away, just when I've got a last chance to get back on the nine?"

"Give it away, you chump! Why the best way to throw 'em off the track, and make 'em feel sure that we had nothing to do with it is to help Bill look for his glasses. Come on. It'll be a joke, but they can't appreciate it."

Somewhat dubious of the plan, Mersfeld followed North, who strolled up to Bill. The Varsity pitcher's face wore a worried look.

"Lose something?" asked North innocently.

"Yes, my glasses. They must have dropped out of my pocket when we were skylarking here."

"That's too bad!" and North winked at Mersfeld. "We'll help you look."

"Sure," agreed the deposed pitcher, and the two hypocrites went carefully over the ground, laughing to themselves as they thought of the glasses in the muzzle of the cannon.

Darkness came and the search had to be given up. Puzzled as to what could have happened to his glasses, uselessly and mechanically feeling in pocket after pocket, Bill accompanied his brothers back to his room. Mersfeld and North went off together.

"Well, what are you going to do?" asked Pete, as he looked at the pitcher.

"I don't know what to do," and Bill's tone was despondent.

"Maybe you can get along without them now, for the few remaining games," suggested Cap.

"No," and Bill shook his head. "I'll need them, for I tried to pitch without them to-day, and my curves were away off. And as for the remaining games—they're the most important of the season. We've just *got* to win them to make good and keep the pennant. I don't see what could have happened to the glasses."

"You might have lost them anywhere between the diamond and here," said Whistle-Breeches. "We'll look again in the morning."

"Say!" cried Pete. "Can't you get some oculist in town to fix you up a pair that will do? It can't be that they were such peculiar glasses that they can't be duplicated."

"Maybe not," half-agreed Bill, "but the old rain-maker-astronomer said the lenses had to be ground in a certain way, and I don't know where he had them made."

"We'll try some one in town," went on Cap. "I believe they can fix you up," and they spent some time talking of that possibility.

Bill was worried, and with good reason. He wanted to maintain his position as pitcher, and he knew he could not do so if he did not "deliver the goods." That he could pitch without the glasses he did not believe, but he was anxious for morning to come that he might test himself again.

Bright and early he and Cap went out to the diamond, not only to look for the glasses but to do some work with the horsehide. It is needless to say that the glasses were not recovered, and to Bill's despair he found that he was throwing wild.

"It won't do," spoke Cap despondently, as he tossed back the ball which he had had to reach away outside of the plate to gather in.

"No, I guess not," agreed his brother. "It's either a new pair of specs for me, or—some one else in the box."

"We'll try to get a new pair of glasses first," suggested Cap, as cheerfully as he could.

An oculist whom they consulted, but not the one to whom they had first gone after the accident, looked grave when he had tested Bill's eyes, and heard the story of the blow.

"Of course I can fit you with glasses," he said, "but it may take some time to get them just right."

"How long?" asked the pitcher anxiously.

"A week—perhaps two."

"It won't do!" declared Bill. "Why the last Sandrim game comes off in three days, and a week later the final with the Tuckerton nine. I've got to pitch in both."

The oculist shrugged his shoulders.

"I'll do my best," he said. "The lenses will have to be specially ground. If I knew where the others were made I could get them from there."

But the astronomer had failed to say where he had had Bill's glasses made, and there was nothing for it but to try some other lens-making place. Meanwhile the oculist said he would temporarily fit Bill with a pair of glasses.

But when the pitcher tried to use them, his curves were worse off than before, and with despair in his heart he laid aside the spectacles.

"I'll have to wait for the others," he said.

"But what about the game with Sandrim?" asked Captain Graydon. "Can you pitch for us?"

Bill shook his head, and said nothing. The captain and coach looked at each other.

"We'll have to put Mersfeld back in the box," decided Mr. Windam dubiously.

"Yes, and he'll have to practice hard every spare minute, and even then—" The captain did not finish, but they knew what he meant.

It was with wild and ill-concealed exultation in his heart that Mersfeld received orders to take his old place.

"Now it's up to you to make good!" said North to him.

"And I'll do it, too!" was the fierce response. "Bill Smith shan't get his hands on the ball again."

Mersfeld began hard and steady practice, and, whether it was that the rest had done him good, or whether he had improved did not develop, but there was a more hopeful look on the faces of the captain and coach.

"We may do Sandrim yet," said Graydon, "and if Bill can get his glasses in time for the Tuckerton game we may pull out ahead."

"I hope so, but it's going to be a hard row to hoe."

Bill and his brothers and friends made strenuous efforts in the little while that remained to get the glasses in time, but there was a delay, the lenses were not ready, and when the day of the final game with Sandrim arrived Mersfeld was in the box.

Bill sat on the bench, bitterness in his heart, his fingers fairly aching to get hold of the ball. But he knew that his eyes were practically useless.

It was a hard game, and Westfield won it only by the hardest kind of work, and the narrow margin of one run. It was due more to the support Mersfeld got than to his pitching that he pulled the contest out of the fire, and at one time, when Sandrim had three men on bases, and none out it looked like a walk-over for them.

But Cap, who was behind the bat, and Pete, at short, were towers of strength, and once more the Smith boys, even though the trio was broken, demonstrated their worth.

"Now, if we can take Tuckerton's scalp we'll be all right," remarked the coach to the captain, as they strolled off the diamond after the game.

"Yes, but we need Bill. Oh, if his eyes would only get right again!"

"Yes, or if he can only get his glasses in time."

It was three days later before the oculist had the special lenses, and Bill tried them hopefully. At first they seemed to be all right, but after he had pitched a few balls Cap called to him:

"Get 'em over a little better, Bill. That last one was quite a ways out."

"What's the matter? Why it went right over the plate!"

Pete who was behind Cap, watching his brother's curves started, and the oldest Smith lad shook his head. Then Bill knew that the glasses were not the same.

"I guess it's all up," he said despondently. "I'm out of it."

"No!" cried Cap. "We'll help you!"

"What can you do?" Bill wanted to know. "There's no use having this oculist try it again."

"No, but we'll find Professor Clatter and Tithonus Somnus and get him to make a right pair of glasses. That's our last chance!"

"And a mighty slim one, too!" murmured Bill, "with the final game only a few days off!"

CHAPTER XXX

BILL'S FALL

W
HEN the oculist learned that the glasses he had made for Bill were practically useless, he wanted to try again, and, as there could be no harm in it, and as some good might result, the pitcher consented. But he and his brothers at once began the task of trying to locate Professor Clatter and his friend the astronomer.

And a task it was, for they had nothing by which to go. The Smith boys knew the towns at which the medicine man usually stopped in his travels, and telegrams were sent to the police of each one, asking them to have Mr. Clatter at once get into communication with his former friends. But the answers that came back stated that the professor had not recently been in the town addressed or else had just left.

The time was getting woefully short. Preparations were completed for the final and deciding game of the series, which as far as the pennant went, was a tie between Tuckerton and Westfield.

With the exception of their pitcher Westfield had the best nine in many years, and her rival was equally well provided for. It would be the hottest game of the season, and indications pointed to record-breaking attendance.

"Oh, if I only could pitch!" sighed poor Bill. "It's the one game of the year."

"And Miss Morton will be there," added Cap.

"Yes, hang it all. Oh, I've a good notion to get some surgeon to operate on me, and see if he can't straighten my eyes!"

"No time for that now," said Pete sadly, for he and his brother, as well as all their friends, sympathized deeply with Bill. "It's hard luck, old man, but it can't be helped."

Mersfeld was practicing early and late, and even Cap, who was to be behind the bat, had to admit that the former twirler was in good form.

"He can't touch you when you are at your best though, Bill," he said to his brother, "and I wish you were going to be in the box, but—"

It now seemed practically sure that no help could be had from Professor Clatter or his odd friend. And the second pair of glasses made by the oculist were worse than the first. Bill's vision was away out of focus when he used them.

"It's me for the bench again," he said the night before the big game, and nothing that his brothers or friends could say consoled him.

A vigorous search was still kept up for the missing case of spectacles, and notices were posted about the school regarding them, but they were still in the cannon, and no one thought of looking there, save the two conspirators, and of course they did not. There was unholy joy between them.

"You got what you wanted," said North to Mersfeld when the make-up of the nine for the concluding championship game was announced the night preceding it.

"That's right, thanks to you."

"Oh, well, I'll depend upon you to help me out, sometime. I've got a score to pay back to Cap Smith yet," and there was a vindictive look on the bully's face.

The Westfield nine went out on the diamond for early practice on the morning of the game, and Mersfeld seemed in good form. There was a confident smile on his face as he threw the balls to Cap.

"Keep it up," advised the catcher, who wished in vain that his big mitt was receiving the swift balls his brother could send in, in place of those from Mersfeld.

"Tuckerton is bringing along two extra pitchers I hear," said the captain to Coach Windam. "They must be looking for a hard game!"

"I hope we give it to 'em! As for box men, we'll put Mersfeld in, of course, and if worst comes to worst and he doesn't last we'll have to rely on Newton."

"I suppose so. Oh, if only Bill Smith—! But what's the use, we'll do the best we can."

It was the afternoon of the great game. Already the grandstands on the Westfield grounds were beginning to fill up with the cohorts of the two schools, and other spectators who came to look on, and cheer. There were pretty girls galore, and a glance over the seats showed a riot of colors from the hats and dresses of the maidens, to the gay banners and ribbons on horns and canes.

The Tuckerton nine had arrived in a big coach, and their entrance on the diamond was a signal for a burst of cheers and many songs.

Then out trotted the home team, and there was a wild burst of barbaric voices in greeting, while rival singing bands, more or less in harmony, chanted the praises of their respective teams.

The Smith boys were with their mates, and, even though he knew he was not going to play, Bill had put on a uniform.

"I'll feel better sitting on the bench than up in the stand," he said to his chums. He tried to smile, but it was a woeful imitation.

There was a sharp practice by both teams. Cap took Mersfeld to a secluded spot, and gave him some final advice about signals, before they started to warm-up. Bill, who wanted to see how his rival was handling the horsehide strolled over to watch him and Cap.

"Pretty good," he said to Mersfeld, who had pitched in some hot ones.

"Glad you think so," was the somewhat ungracious answer. "I guess I'll do." Mersfeld was anything but modest.

It was almost time for the game to be called. Just back of where Bill was watching his brother and Mersfeld, Whistle-Breeches was knocking grounders to Pete, who was to play shortstop. Some one threw in a ball from the outfield to one of the fungle batters. The sphere went wild, and came toward Whistle-Breeches.

"Look out!" yelled Pete, and Anderson raised his bat intending to stop the wildly-thrown horsehide. He hit it harder than he intended, and it was shunted off in the direction of Bill.

"Duck!" suddenly exclaimed Cap, who saw his brother's danger, and instinctively Bill dodged. He turned to one side so quickly that he lost his balance, and the next moment he fell heavily, his head striking the ground with considerable force, while the ball landed some distance from him.

They all expected to see Bill jump to his feet with a laugh at his awkwardness, but to the surprise of all he remained lying there, still and quiet.

"Bill's hurt!" cried Cap, making a dash toward him, while several other players came hurrying forward to see what was the matter.

CHAPTER XXXI

"PLAY BALL!"

Cap Smith was the first to reach his brother. As he lifted him up Bill opened his eyes.

"I'm all right," he murmured. "I can stand alone."

He proved it by doing so. His hand went to his head, and when it came away there was a little smear of blood on the palm.

"Must have hit on a stone and cut myself," he said, a bit faintly. "But I'm all right now."

"Are you sure?" asked Pete, slipping his arm around his brother. "Better come over here and sit down."

He led Bill to the bench, and indeed the pitcher was a trifle dizzy, and his head felt queer, for he had fallen harder than he had supposed.

The other players, finding that nothing serious was the matter went back to their practice. In the grandstands the singing and cheering was multiplied. Crowds of pretty girls, eager youths, demure chaperones, old grads, young grads and mere spectators continued to arrive until every seat was filled.

"It's going to be a great game," murmured Cap, who, finding that his brother was apparently all right, resumed, his catching with Mersfeld. "I never saw such a crowd!"

"It's money in the treasury whether we win the pennant or not," declared J. Evans Green, the business-like manager.

"But we *are* going to win!" declared Cap emphatically. "Keep 'em guessing, Mersfeld, and you'll do. Now when I put three fingers on my mitt so, let me have a swift drop," and he went on with his code of signals.

Those Smith Boys on the Diamond

The conferences between the respective captains had ended, and Burke, head of the Tuckerton Varsity nine, signalled to his men to come in from practice, as they were to bat first. Graydon assembled his team for a few final instructions.

"Sorry you're not playing with us to-day," he said to poor Bill, who was sitting on the bench. The cut in his head had stopped bleeding.

"You're no more sorry than I am," declared the pitcher ruefully. "But it can't be helped."

"We may have to call on you yet," said the coach, "if they knock Mersfeld and Newton out of the box."

"I'm afraid I couldn't do much good," was Bill's doleful answer.

"Play ball!" howled the umpire, and the players took their places, Mersfeld catching the new white horsehide sphere the official tossed to him.

The first ball which Mersfeld delivered was cleanly hit away out in centrefield, and when it came back the batter was on second base. There was a wild riot of cheers at this auspicious opening for Tuckerton, and a grim look on the faces of the Westfield players.

"That looks bad," murmured Bill, as he watched Mersfeld wind up for his next delivery. The pitcher was visibly nervous, and Cap, seeing it, made an excuse to walk out to him.

"Keep cool!" he whispered, "or you won't last."

Mersfeld stiffened, and struck out the next man. But the third one got a three bagger out of him, and the following one a single. When the inning came to a close there were three runs chalked up for the rivals of our friends, and there was only gloom for the home team. Nor was it dissipated by the triumphant songs their opponents sang.

One run was the best that Graydon's men could do on their first trial, though captain and coach pleaded earnestly with them.

"I guess they've got our number," murmured Pete to his brother as the latter donned his protector and mask.

"Oh, don't be so gloomy," was the advice.

Mersfeld went from bad to worse, and at the beginning of the fourth inning the captain and coach held a consultation.

"We've got to do something," said Graydon.

"I agree with you. But what?"

"Newton will have to go in."

"It looks so. We can't chance Bill."

"No. Well, tell Newton to pitch next inning." Two more runs went to the credit of Tuckerton, making the score eight to two in their favor.

By desperate playing and taking several chances our friends managed to pull a brace of tallies out of the ruck that inning, so that there was some hope. Mersfeld sulked when told to go to the bench, and pleaded for another chance, but the coach and captain were firm.

"Get ready, Newton," ordered Graydon.

The substitute Varsity twirler was not a wonder, and he knew it, but he started off well, and there was some hope, until he began to go to pieces after issuing passes to two men. Then it seemed all up with him, though only one run went to Tuckerton's credit that inning.

Cap shook his head dubiously when he took off his mask at the beginning of the second half of the fifth inning. His apprehensive feeling was shared by his teammates, by the coach, the manager and by thousands of the Westfield supporters, who sat in gloomy silence while the cohorts of Tuckerton yelled, shouted and sang themselves hoarse.

"I'm going to do something desperate," declared the coach, to the captain, when two runs had come in to sweeten the tally for Westfield, thereby causing wild hope among her friends.

"What are you going to do?" asked Graydon.

"I know we can beat these fellows, even now, if we could only hold them down to no more runs," went on Windam. "And to shut them out for the rest of the game we need a good pitcher. Mersfeld can't do it, Newton doesn't count, Bill is out of it, and I'm going to put in Morgan."

"What! The Freshman sub?"

"It's a last hope, I know," admitted the coach, "but we've got to do something. Morgan is good, and if he can last he'll be all right."

Rather listlessly, and almost hopelessly the captain consented to it. He was crossing to tell Morgan of the decision arrived at, when he noticed that Cap and Bill were having a little warm-up practice off to one side, for it would not be Cap's turn to bat in some time.

As Bill stung in a ball his brother uttered a cry of surprise.

"What's the matter—hurt?" asked the captain quickly, fearing more bad luck. With his best catcher laid off, as well as the star pitcher, the game might as well be given up.

"Hurt! No, I'm not hurt," answered Cap. "Here, Bill just throw a few more that way," he called eagerly to his brother.

Bill, wondering what was up, did so, fairly stinging them in with his old-time force. The look of surprise on Cap's face grew.

"Here!" he called to the captain, and he motioned for Bill to approach. "Do you notice any difference in your eyes?" he asked his brother eagerly.

"My eyes?" repeated Bill, slowly.

"His eyes," murmured the captain.

"Yes," went on the catcher. "Every ball you threw came in as straight as a die, and the curve broke just at the right time. Say, maybe I'm loony, or dreaming, but you pitch just as you used to, Bill, before you got hurt! Do your eyes feel any differently?"

"Well, they don't ache as they used to when I pitched without my glasses, and there seems to be a queer feeling in my head." He put his hand back to where he had fallen on the stone a little while before.

"Bill, you've got your eyesight back!" cried Cap eagerly. "I'm sure of it!"

"Do you really believe it?" asked the pitcher trembling with suppressed hope.

"Sure. But we'll try once more. Come over here."

The game was going rather slow now, for the Tuckerton pitcher was tiring, and was not sure of his man. He had decided to walk him, and to kill time was playing with Whistle-Breeches, who was on second. Consequently little attention needed to be given to the contest for the moment by the captain. He could see what Cap and Bill were going to do.

Once more Bill threw in the balls. They came just as they had formerly done, perfectly.

"You'll do!" cried Cap in delight.

"Get ready to go to the box!" ordered the captain tensely.

"But I—I don't understand," stammered the pitcher.

"You've got your sight back!" went on his brother, "and I believe what did it was the fall you just had. It did something to your head—relieved the blood or nerve pressure or something. Anyhow you can pitch once more!"

"That's the stuff!" cried Graydon. "We need you!"

There was a wild yell from the grandstands, and out burst a chorus of a Westfield song.

"Whistle-Breeches brought in a run," cried Graydon. "Things are picking up! Now we'll wallop 'em!"

Three runs were the best Westfield could do that inning and when the home team was ready to take the field there was a murmur of surprise as it was announced that Bill Smith would pitch.

As Bill started toward the box there was some excitement at one of the entrance gates near the grandstand back of the home plate.

"I must go in! I must go in!" a voice cried. "I tell you the Smith boys need me!"

Something in the voice attracted the attention of Bill, Cap and Pete. They looked, and saw Professor Clatter rush past a ticket-taker.

"Here I am!" cried the medicine man. "I came on as soon as I could. I got your message in Langfield. And here are your glasses, Bill!"

He held up the case containing the missing spectacles, and fairly ran across the diamond.

CHAPTER XXXII

NIP AND TUCK FOR VICTORY

THE game was halted. There were angry demands from several players as to why a stranger was allowed to come on the field. Others, recognizing the professor, clamored that it was all right.

"I came as soon as I could!" explained the medicine man to the Smith boys, who gathered about him. "I knew something must be wrong. I can't locate Tithonus though. What is it? Bill's glasses? Here they are, found in the most opportune way! Talk about golden rivers!"

The professor was panting from his run and his rapid talk. He held the glasses to Bill.

"Where did you find them?" gasped the pitcher.

"Just now, as I was coming across the campus. I left my wagon over in the road. As I was passing one of the cannon some of the janitors were cleaning it. There was a lot of leaves and rubbish in it. Then out fell the glasses just as I passed. I grabbed them up, and I knew the whole story."

"You knew the whole story?" cried Cap. "Who put them there?"

"No, no! I can't tell that!" declared Mr. Clatter, while North and Mersfeld looked at each other in relief. "I mean I understand it all—about your messages to me," went on the medicine man. "At first I couldn't imagine why you had telegraphed me. I knew you must be in some kind of trouble though."

"Yes, we generally are," murmured Pete.

"And, as soon as I saw the glasses fall from the cannon I realized what it was. Bill lost them, perhaps a bird took them for its nest. At any rate here they are, and it's very lucky, too, for I can't get any trace of Tithy. Here, Bill, put them on and play ball."

"I don't need them now," answered the pitcher.

"Don't need them! You don't mean to say that the game is over—you haven't lost the championship; have you?" and the professor looked pained, for he was a lover of base ball, and in his journeyings he faithfully read the accounts of the games at Westfield, where his friends the Smith boys attended. "Have you lost the pennant?" asked the professor sadly.

"Not yet, but we're in a fair way to if this keeps on," murmured Cap, for the score was seven to nine in favor of Tuckerton.

"But why doesn't Bill need his glasses then?" asked Mr. Clatter.

"Because I can see to pitch without them," answered our hero. "A funny thing just happened, Professor," and Bill told about his fall and the odd effect it had had on his vision. The traveling medicine man looked interested.

"Yes, that's exactly how it may have taken place," he declared, as Cap stated his theory. "Here, let me have a look at you, Bill."

"Say," angrily cried Burke, captain of the Tuckerton nine, "if this is a ball game let's go on with it, and if it's a hospital for injured players we'll get off the field."

"That's right," added Hedden, the pitcher. "We're here to win the pennant, not to listen to fairy stories."

"Play ball!" yelled Brower, the catcher.

"Easy now," counseled Professor Clatter. "It won't take me but a moment to look at Bill's head, and then the game can go on. You don't seem to realize that something extraordinary has taken place here."

"It will be extraordinary if we ever play ball again," remarked Burke, sarcastically. But the professor did not heed him. He was looking at the cut on Bill's head.

"That accounts for your eyes getting right again," he said. "It's a bad cut, but you're in shape to play, in spite of it. Go in, and win!"

"That's what we're going to do!" declared Cap.

"Surest thing you know!" cried Pete.

"I'd like to find out how my glasses got in that cannon," spoke Bill, but no one enlightened him, though Professor Clatter, as he looked at the guilty, flushed face of Mersfeld had a suspicion of the truth.

"Play ball!" called the umpire, and the Westfield nine went to their places in the field. Mersfeld, with a bitter look on his face, watched Bill go to the box.

And the pitcher did not need his glasses, though he took them with him as a matter of precaution. With his eyes right once more, and feeling full of confidence Bill exchanged a few preliminary balls with Cap. Then he signified that he was ready for the batter. Cap, with a gratified smile, had noticed that the horsehide cut the plate cleanly and yet the curves broke just at the right time.

"Strike one!" called the umpire suddenly, following the first ball Bill delivered. The batter started. He had not moved his stick. He gave the umpire an indignant glance, opened his mouth as if to say something, and then thought better of it.

There was a long-drawn sigh of relief from the grandstands and bleachers where the Westfield supporters sat, and Bob Chapin ventured to start the song, "We've Got Their Scalp Locks Now!"

Bill smiled at his brother behind the plate. Pete picked up a handful of gravel and tossed it into the air before settling back ready for whatever might come his way.

"Strike two!" came sharply from the umpire.

"That's the way to do it! Make him fan, Bill!" cried Whistle-Breeches.

"He's done," called Bob Chapin.

"Make him give you a nice one," was the advice the batter got from his friends.

The man with the stick tapped the plate and smiled confidently. He was still smiling when the next ball came. He struck at it—missed it clean, and threw his bat to the ground with such force as to splinter it.

"Batter's out!" said the umpire quietly.

"That's the way to do it!"

"There's more where those came from!"

"We've got their Angora!"

These were the cries that greeted Bill's initial effort in the box at that championship game. Matters were looking brighter for Westfield, and every man on the team, and every supporter who wanted to see the pennant stay where it was, felt hope coming back to him.

There was a little apprehension in Tuckerton's ranks. The game had seemed so sure to them, but now the tide was turning. Still Bill might not be able to keep it up.

As for our hero, however, he knew that his eye was as true as it had ever been, and he felt able to go on for nine innings if necessary. But only four remained in which to turn the trick. Could he do it? Others beside himself asked that question.

The next man stepped to the plate. Two fouls and a miss on the last strike was the best he could do, and he went back to the bench. The third man Bill struck out cleanly.

"Wow! Wow!" howled the Westfield crowd. "We've got 'em going!"

But it was to be no easy victory. Though by reason of Bill's twirling a momentary halt had been called on the winning streak of the visitors, still Westfield must make more runs in order to win the game.

And this was not easy. Hedden was hit for two singles, but the Westfield players were a bit careless on bases, and one was caught napping. One run was brought in on Cap's three bagger making the score eight to nine, with a single leading tally in favor of the visitors.

Those Smith Boys on the Diamond

From then on it was nip and tuck for victory. Bill kept up the good twirling, and such box work as he exhibited was not seen for many a long day on the Westfield diamond. Not a Tuckerton player got a hit off him in the next three innings, goose eggs going up in the frames, that up to the advent of Bill had contained at least one tally for each time the visitors were at bat.

But, on the other hand Westfield, try as they did, could not score. The captain and coach begged and pleaded, and the crowds by songs and cheers urged their men to battle to the death. It seemed useless. The two teams, now evenly matched, sea-sawed back and forth, with grim, bulldog tenacity, but there the game hung in the balance.

Tuckerton was still one run ahead when they came to bat in the ninth inning.

"Hold 'em down! Hold 'em down!" pleaded Cap to Bill.

"I will," promised the pitcher, and he did, striking three men out in quick succession amid the cheers of the crowd.

"Now's our last chance," murmured Captain Graydon as his men came in. "It's do or die for the pennant now!"

CHAPTER XXXIII

WINNING THE PENNANT

"ONE run to tie, two to win and three to make a good job of it," murmured Cap, as he walked to the bench with his brothers. "Can we do it?"

"We've got to," answered Bill.

"You make a home run, I'll limp along after you, and Pete can follow," suggested Bill. "That will do the business."

"It might happen," said Cap. "Whistle-Breeches is up first, then I follow, and, after Graydon has a whack, you and Pete come along, Bill."

"Oh, don't talk about it!" exclaimed the pitcher. "It makes me nervous," but he did not show any signs of it.

"How are your eyes?" asked Pete.

"All right. I feel fine. But I'd like to know who hid my glasses."

"Batter up!" called the umpire, and Whistle-Breeches, a little pale because of what depended on his work, walked to the plate.

"Now line out a good one!" counseled the coach. "You can do it. Wait for a nice one."

It was good advice, and well meant, but alas! Whistle-Breeches fanned the air.

"One down!" exulted the captain of the Tuckerton nine. "We only need two more!"

"Well, you don't get me!" murmured Cap, with a grim tightening of his mouth. And he made good. A pretty two-bagger was his contribution, and he got to third on a little fly which Graydon knocked, but the captain was out at first.

"Two down, play for the batter!" called Burke. "They've only got one chance, and they can't make good. The pennant comes to Tuckerton!"

"Don't you fool yourself," murmured Bill, as he went to the plate. Hedden, his rival pitcher, regarded him with a mocking smile. Bill was not especially strong in stick work, but somehow he felt that he was going to make good to-day.

He saw a ball coming, and sized it up for a slow out. Knowing the peculiarity of the curve which Hedden pitched Bill stepped right into it. His bat met the horsehide squarely, and with a "Ping!" that sent a thrill of joy not only to his heart but to the hearts of his brothers and friends.

"Right on the nose! Oh, what a poke!" cried Whistle-Breeches who rejoiced for Bill over what he himself could not do.

Away sailed the ball, well over the centre fielder's head, away sped Bill legging it for first with all the speed of which he was capable.

"Run! Run! Run!"

"Come on in, Cap!"

"Oh what a poke!"

"Pretty! Pretty!"

The crowd on the stands was yelling and jumping up and down. Old men were tossing their hats into the air, clapping each other on the back, making friends with strangers, and telling each other that it reminded them of the time when they were boys.

Bill swung around second, as Cap fairly leaped over home plate, bringing in the tying run. The Tuckerton players were wild with chagrin. The game was being pulled out of the fire—snatched from them at the moment when they thought they saw a safe victory. The centre fielder nearly had the ball now, and Bill was heading for third base.

"Go on! Go on!"

"Home! Home!"

This and other advice was shouted at him. He gave a quick glance around, and decided that he would risk it by going on to the last bag. It was a narrow chance, almost too narrow, and Bill had to slide so far that his uniform took on a new shade, and his mouth and eyes were filled with dust and gravel, for the ball whizzed into the hands of the eager baseman.

"Safe!" decided the umpire after a breathless run to third that he might see the outcome.

The score was now tied!

There was a howl of disgust from the Tuckerton crowd but the decision stood, and there was wild rejoicing on the part of the Westfield throng.

"Now then, Pete, it's up to you," said the coach solemnly as the third member of the Smith boys trio stepped to the bat. "If you don't bring Bill in at least, I'll never speak to you again."

"I'll do my best," declared the doughty little shortstop. He was one of the best men who could have been up in an emergency of this kind, with two out, a man on third and the winning run still needed. For Pete was as cool as the proverbial cucumber.

He smiled in a tantalizing fashion at the Tuckerton pitcher, who was on the verge of a nervous breakdown because of the many epithets hurled at him, in an endeavor to "get his goat." He had to watch Bill carefully, for that worthy was playing off as far as he dared, hoping to slip in with the needed winning run. The catcher, too, was fearful lest some ball get by him, and had told the pitcher to be on the alert to run in instantly in the event of a passed ball.

"Ball one!" howled the umpire, as Hedden threw.

"Oh wow! He's going to walk you, Pete!" called Graydon.

"You've got a pass!" shouted Bob Chapin.

Those Smith Boys on the Diamond

Pete smiled cheerfully. He thought the next ball looked good, and swung at it, but he had been fooled by a neat trick.

"Strike one!" said the umpire, and a breathless silence followed.

"Two more like that and we've got 'em!" called the catcher to Hedden. "You can do it."

The pitcher nodded. He threw the swiftest ball of which he was capable. It came almost before Pete was ready for it, but with the quickness of light he swung on it.

Oh what a "Ping!" followed, and he knew that he had made good. Once more, amid the frenzied howls of the crowd, the ball sailed outward and upward.

"Bill, Oh Bill! Where are you? Come in! Come in!" pleaded scores to him. But the pitcher did not need these entreaties. On he came running as he had never run before. The catcher, to disconcert him, stood as though to catch the ball. Bill dared not look around to make sure that it had not been caught and thrown home. Brower was right in his path.

"Slide!" some one called to him, and for the second time that day Bill dropped and shot forward on the ground. His hand touched the plate, and he knew that he was safe, for he had not heard the thud of the ball in the catcher's mitt. Then, he felt some heavy body fall on him, and for the moment the breath was knocked from him, and he lost consciousness. He had knocked the catcher's feet from under him, and toppled that player in the dust.

Cap ran to pick up his brother.

"Hurt?" he cried anxiously. "Oh Bill, you did it! We win."

"No—n-not much hurt!" gasped Bill. "Just—just a little—little short—of wind—that's all."

They gave him water and he felt better, and then he looked out over the diamond. Pete had reached third, and was still running. Around the last bag he swung, but the right fielder far on amid the daisies had the ball now.

"Go back! Go back!" howled Graydon, for, though the game was won he wanted to pile up another run against Tuckerton if he could.

But Pete did not heed. The ball had been thrown, but the fielder had to run so far back for it, that he could not get it far enough in. There was just a chance for Pete to make a home run, and he took that chance.

The horsehide fell short of the second baseman, who ran to get it. By this time Pete was half way home, and running well.

"Come on! Come on!" pleaded hundreds to him, and Pete came.

"Slide!" cried the coach, and, as Bill had done, so did Pete, but with more cause.

On came the ball, thrown swiftly by the second baseman. Pete was hurtling forward through a cloud of dust, his hand eagerly stretched out to feel the plate. His fingers touched it, and a welcome thrill ran through him, just as he heard the thud of the ball in the catcher's glove. Down came the horsehide on his shoulder with vicious force.

"How's it?" excitedly yelled the catcher to the umpire.

There was a moment's silence, and the players and crowd hardly breathed. It seemed as if the weight of kingdoms hung on the decision, and Pete lay there waiting.

"Safe!" decided the umpire, and yells of delight mingled with those of chagrin. Westfield had the game now by two runs and the pennant remained with them.

Oh what rejoicing there was! No need to play the game out farther. Indeed it could scarcely have been done had the coach or captain desired it, so wild with delight were the members of the nine.

"Oh you Smith boys!" was the gladsome cry, and around our heroes there danced a wild and enthusiastic mob of players of the game. Horns tooted, rattles added their din, old men, youths and maidens swelled the riot with their voices, the shrill tones of the girls sounding high above the hoarser notes of triumph.

"We win! We win!" cried Graydon, hugging the rather grave and sedate coach, and whirling him about in a dance.

"Yes, and at the last minute," added Mr. Windam. "That was a lucky fall of Bill Smith's."

"There was crooked work somewhere," said the captain in a low voice. "Those glasses never fell into the cannon, and I know whom to suspect."

"Then keep it to yourself," advised the coach, and Graydon did so.

It seemed impossible that it was all over, that the school baseball season was at an end, and that Westfield still had the pennant, yet such was the case. Already the crowds were leaving the grandstands. Students were gathering in groups to cheer over, or sing about, the victory. The team was hugged and hustled here and there. The Smith boys and their mates were lifted to the shoulders of their fellows and paraded about the diamond. The Tuckertons had given a cheer for the victors, and, in turn, had been cheered for their plucky fight.

"And to think that this is the end of the season," remarked Bill regretfully to his brothers, as they walked over toward the gymnasium.

"Oh, but it will soon be fall, and then for the good old pigskin punts!" exclaimed Pete.

"That's so. I wonder if we can make the eleven?" said Cap. "I hope we can."

"We'll try, anyhow," declared Bill.

How they tried, and with what success they had will be told of in the third volume of this series to be called "Those Smith Boys on the Gridiron; or A Touchdown in Time." In that book we will meet with our school friends again, and learn how they played several great games.

As Bill and his brothers strolled across the campus they saw a group of girls coming toward them.

Those Smith Boys on the Diamond

"Oh cats!" exclaimed Bill. "I look like sin; don't I?"

"I've seen you cleaner," answered Whistle-Breeches, as he noted Bill's torn jacket and dusty trousers. "But what's the odds?"

"There's Miss Morton," murmured the pitcher.

"Oh!" cried the girl, with whom he had once rode at such top speed to play in the Freshman game. "Oh, I want to shake hands with all you boys! Wasn't it perfectly splendid?"

"Glad you think so!" mumbled Bill, trying to hide behind Cap. But Miss Morton would have none of that. She held out her hand to Bill especially.

"I'll spoil your gloves!" he protested.

"As if I cared for them!" and she only laughed at the grimy stains which Bill made on the white kids. Then, in turn she and the other young ladies greeted our friends, and repeated, over and over again, in more or less emphatic words, what they thought of the victory.

"And may I add a word," spoke a voice, as the girls moved off. The boys turned to behold Professor Clatter.

"It was fine!" he declared. "Not even by the use if my Rapid Robust Resolute Resolvent, my Peerless, Permanent Pain Preventive or my Spotless Saponifier could a more noble victory have been won. I congratulate you. Pactolus congratulates you, and when we find the golden river we'll make a crown of victory for you. But what I want to add most especially is, that our mutual friend Tithonus Somnus has just arrived. His wagon is over near mine, and he and I entreat you to come and see us, and partake of such humble fare as we may afford."

"Do you mean all of us?" asked Cap.

"The entire nine!" cried the medicine man warmly. "We will dine out of doors, and Mercurio will serve the viands."

"What say, fellows; shall we go?" asked Cap, for the members of the Varsity team were gathered about the Smith boys.

"Go? Of course," answered Graydon. "We can break training now, and we'll eat golden rivers or Resolute Resolvent or even Spotless Saponifiers! Lead on!"

"You say Tithy has arrived?" asked Bill, as the little throng moved over the campus, it having been arranged that as soon as they got off their uniforms they would go to the professor's wagon.

"Yes, he heard that I was headed here, and followed."

"What business is he in now?" inquired Pete.

"Oh, he is selling a wonderful instrument. It is a pocket knife, a glass cutter, a can opener, hammer, screw driver, and twenty-six other tools, more or less, combined into one. Tithy is enthusiastic over it. Well, I'll go to tell him you are coming, and then I will bid Mercurio set the table."

The professor, with a low bow, turned away, and hastened off.

"Queer chap," commented Graydon.

"But as good as gold," added Bill, and his brothers agreed with him. "To think of him finding my glasses. I wonder how they got there?"

No one answered him, and Mersfeld and North did not hear the question. Perhaps they would not have replied had they listened to it.

A little later the members of the nine were seated in the shade of the two queer wagons, on the long, green grass, beside the road, partaking of the hospitality of Professor Clatter and Tithonus Somnus, who gravely announced that he had changed his name, as well as his trade and that thenceforth he would be known as Cornelius Cutaby.

Proudly he showed the new implement for which he was traveling agent.

"It will do anything from cutting glass to taking an automobile apart," he declared.

"Well, if it will open some more of that ginger ale, I'll be glad of it," remarked Bill. "These olives and ham sandwiches make me thirsty."

"What ho! Mercurio!" called Professor Clatter. "Pass the ginger ale," and, having executed his own command he opened the bottles with the combined glass cutter and screw driver, and served to his friends the frothing beverage.

"Now fellows, for the baseball song—'Strike 'em Out and Run 'em Down!' and then we'll go back to school and get ready for the celebration to-night!" suggested Cap, after a pause.

The improvised banquet was over. In the twilight the boys stood up, and softly sang the time-honored song of Westfield, sung whenever there was a victory. Professor Clatter brought out a guitar and played the accompaniment, and Tithy—I beg his pardon, Cornelius Cutaby—joined in the chorus.

And now, for a time, we will take leave of Those Smith Boys, though if the fates are kind, they may be met with again, as well as the professor and the traveling agent for the combined glass cutter and monkey wrench.

THE END

Boy Inventors' Series

The author knows these subjects from a practical standpoint. Each book is printed from new plates on a good quality of paper and bound in cloth. Each book wrapped in a jacket printed in colors.

Price 60c each

1....Boy Inventors' Wireless Triumph

2....Boy Inventors' and the Vanishing Sun

3....Boy Inventors' Diving Torpedo Set

4....Boy Inventors' Flying Ship

5....Boy Inventors' Electric Ship

6....Boy Inventors' Radio Telephone

The "How-to-do-it" Books

These books teach the use of tools; how to sharpen them; to design and layout work. Printed from new plates and bound in cloth. Profusely illustrated. Each book is wrapped in a printed jacket.

Price $1.00 each

1....Carpentry for Boys

2....Electricity for Boys

3....Practical Mechanics for Boys

For Sale by all Book-sellers, or sent postpaid on receipt of the above price.

M · A · DONOHUE · & · COMPANY
711 · SOUTH · DEARBORN · STREET · · CHICAGO